A LITTLE REBELLION

A LITTLE REBELLION

BRIDGET MORAN

ARSENAL PULP PRESS
Vancouver, B.C.

ARSENAL PULP PRESS
100-1062 Homer Street
Vancouver, B.C.
Canada V6B 2W9

The Publisher gratefully acknowledges the assistance of the Canada Council and the Cultural Services Branch, B.C. Ministry of Tourism and Minister Responsible for Culture.

Edited by Linda Field
Typeset by the Vancouver Desktop Publishing Centre
Printed and bound in Canada by Kromar Printing

CANADIAN CATALOGUING IN PUBLICATION DATA:

Moran, Bridget, 1923-
    A little rebellion

    ISBN 0-88978-252-0

    1. Moran, Bridget, 1923- 2. Social workers—British Columbia—
Biography. 3. Social service—British Columbia—History. I. Title.
HV40.32.M67A3 1992   361.3'2'092   C92-091635-X

This book is dedicated to the memory

of my courageous Irish mother,

Rose Anne Drugan 1890-1975

"I hold that a little rebellion, now and then, is a good thing, and as necessary in the political world as storms in the physical."

—THOMAS JEFFERSON
in a letter to James Madison, 1787

PROLOGUE

On November 4, 1951, as I stepped off the train into a fog-filled morning on Cordova Street in Vancouver, fatigued and a bit dizzy, I thought, "I wonder what the future holds for me here in British Columbia?" I had just completed three days and three nights sitting in a coach on the Canadian Pacific Railway. I had said goodbye to Toronto, my mother, my brother and sisters, to my university career, and to the friends I had made over the years. As the train rattled its way along the icy tracks I had watched a large part of Canada disappear behind me like a wintery grey ribbon, and in those long hours spent gazing out of the train window, I thought about the past and pondered my future.

I was twenty-eight years old and already I had had a variety of careers: country school teacher in Saskatchewan, a two-year stint in the Women's Royal Canadian Naval Service during the Second World War, five years and some months attending the University of Toronto, at the same time working as a cashier, a waitress, an elevator operator, and in the summer months, a cabin girl in a fishing resort in northern Ontario.

Like the rest of humanity there were many sides to my nature. Perhaps because of my Irish heritage I was gregarious, fond of parties, singing, dancing, and keeping long hours. Balancing this almost excessive sociability I was an avid student and a lover of books. I was also a political creature, ready at the drop of a hat to debate the need for social justice, economic democracy, or the peace movement. In common with many other Canadians the poverty which had plagued my childhood during the Dirty Thirties had forged my political creed; that creed also owed much to the fact that the world in which I grew up was nearly as male-dominated as it had been two hundred years before when the Earl of Chesterfield wrote, "Women then are only children of a larger growth."

In 1937, I was fourteen years old and one of five children in the Drugan family in the village of Success, Saskatchewan when my father died in Qu'Appelle Sanitorium after a long bout with tuberculosis. For years before his death and for some years afterwards, my family survived on the bounty of Mother Welfare, or what in those days was called relief. Years later I did a little mental arithmetic and reckoned that during the Depression years my mother had received ten cents a day to feed and clothe me. With the Second World War engulfing much of the world, I put on the king's uniform and suddenly the government came up with $1.10 per day as my basic wage along with food, shelter, medical, transportation, and all the perks that went along with being in the military. I had never been able to reconcile the difference between those two figures: ten cents a day as opposed to one dollar and ten cents plus many fringe benefits.

Growing up as I did with my parents' stories of Ireland's struggle for independence and with my personal experience of the poverty syndrome, I do not remember a time in my life when I did not believe that poverty and war and discrimination of every kind were the three greatest evils in the world. My studies in philosophy, literature and history during my years at university only served to reinforce the judgements I had reached earlier through more personalized experience.

I was also politicized by my experiences as a female in a world that seemed to carry the warning, 'For Men Only.' The limited career choices I had as a girl, my lack of sexual freedom compared with my brother and my male friends and the inhibitions which resulted from these restraints, the not-so-subtle social pressures to marry—I had never ever wanted to be a man but I passionately wanted to share some of the freedoms men enjoyed.

My view of the world as male-dominated took a great leap forward in 1950 when I graduated from the University of Toronto with a gold medal and first class honours in Philosophy, English and History. I wanted to continue my studies in history with a view to teaching at the college or university level. As a veteran I was guaranteed one month's financial support at a university for every month I served in the armed forces. Beyond this time limit the Department of Veterans Affairs continued to give financial support if the veteran achieved high second- or first-class marks. I expected that in view of my academic success the department would automatically continue to support me in graduate school—after all, hundreds of other veterans had received just such an extension. It came as a shock to me to discover that Veterans Affairs had conducted an investigation into university history departments across Canada and that the fruits of this investigation did not bode well for me. Their survey disclosed, said the poltroons in Ottawa, that there was no female history professor in any Canadian university or college. This being so, they would be glad to continue to support me if I decided to go into teaching, nursing, or, in a pinch, social work or psychology. I said "Thanks but no thanks," or words to that effect, and stumbled along with my historical studies for another year and some months. As I struggled to find money for books and streetcar fare, I watched fellow students, often men with their second-class marks, continue their studies in the faculties of their choice, supported by the same government department which had turned me down.

Two months into my second year as a graduate history student, I had had enough. I gave the whole thing up. I hopped a Canadian Pacific train and headed for Vancouver and the sanctuary of a younger sister's home.

I was not prepared for the size and the marvelous variety I found in British Columbia when I first arrived in Vancouver. In an atlas, with its brown and green shadings, it looks like any other area in the vast expanse of North America. Far from this sameness, this similarity, however, I discovered a province with a land mass of over one-third million square miles, stretching from the Yukon border in the north through a whole series of snow-capped mountain ranges, turbulent rivers and pristine lakes, through wide valleys and finally on to the ocean with its islands and tides and inlets cut deep into the land.

Soon after my arrival I was hired as a social worker with the provincial government and in that capacity I went from offices in the Fraser Valley and the Okanagan into the Cariboo. As I moved from one region to another, I discovered that I had a romance going with this piece of Canada that was probably going to stay with me as long as I lived. In short, I fell in love with British Columbia.

But as sometimes happens when one is in love, the bond develops complexities with the passage of years and, almost unnoticed, something akin to a love-hate relationship tempers that affection. So it was with me and my adopted province. Things inanimate, the mountains and rivers and the dark reaches of forest, never failed to touch me, to awaken in me a desire to lose myself in their mysteries. Nature itself never failed me. But as the years went by I found that there was another side to British Columbia, a side which filled me first with frustration and despair, and finally anger.

As I attempted to understand what there was in this province that darkened my affection, the phrase 'Two Nations,' which Benjamin Disraeli coined in his novel *Sybil*, often occurred to me—the Two Nations of the rich and the poor. I had always been aware of the existence of these Two Nations in Canada and I took it for granted that they were flourishing in British Columbia as well. So it was not this division of society into the haves and have-nots which haunted me . . . no, it was something else, something more.

A few months after my arrival in the west, the Liberal/Conservative government known as the Coalition was tossed out by the voters and a new business-oriented conservative coalition, the Social Credit, took over management of the province. That management continued for almost four decades except for a three-year break in the 1970s when the New Democratic Party formed the government. I came to realize that the 'something more' which haunted me was the gradual refinement by the Social Credit Party of Disraeli's Two Nations of rich and poor into the infinitely more subtle Two Nations of the powerful and the powerless.

As roads were built, rivers diverted, lands flooded and people who had lived on those lands from time immemorial found themselves disposed, I worked with that other nation, the powerless, in its struggle to survive in British Columbia. Survival was not easy. The governments led by the Bennetts, father and son, and by Bill Vander Zalm after them, had little of generosity or compassion in them. Mega-projects such as Alcan, the Columbia-Peace power projects, instant towns like Tumber Ridge, Expo '86, and the Coquihalla Highway, took precedence over public housing, treatment centres for disturbed children and adults, programs to alleviate poverty, and alternatives to the desperate conditions of the aboriginal people on and off reservations.

A kind of cult of the powerful has permeated the records of those Social Credit years. Pictured as larger than life, the careers and times of W.A.C. Bennett, his son Bill, Bill Vander Zalm, Phil Gaglardi, Ray Williston, Robert Bonner, Ben Ginter, Axel Wenner Gren, Grace McCarthy, the Smiths, Jim Pattison, and dozens of other high profile names, all of them dedicated to the manipulation of capital and the wielding of power, are documented to the exclusion of that other nation—the unemployed, the aged, the single mothers, the aboriginals, the children—in a word, the powerless among us.

Because I was aware of the role of the powerful in recorded provincial history, it came as no surprise to me to discover that the events in which I played a part during the Social Credit years are not given the merest mention, despite the fact that they made headlines for months, involved politicians of every persuasion in adversarial positions, and mobilized individuals and groups in calls for government action. Pages, whole chapters in the publications covering the Social Credit era, are devoted to the building of the Bennett Dam or the manipulation of bonds or the struggle for control of the province's hydroelectric system; in those same publications it is as if the welfare controversy that surfaced in the province in 1964 never happened.

And yet despite that curtain of silence there was such a controversy.

A Little Rebellion is as much about the powerless and my life among them as a social worker in British Columbia as it is about the events of 1964. It documents my early optimism as an eager employee of the welfare department and the gradual erosion of that optimism as right-wing policy and practice destroyed a once proud and progressive welfare system, and describes the attempts of myself and others to cope with a social service milieu which produced problems nearly as often as it solved them until finally the problems began to feed on themselves. It chronicles one small attempt to change the system from within, an attempt which, though not recorded in official histories, had a marked effect on the course of my life.

ONE

How to describe the aura of Vancouver when I walked out of the CPR station that November day in 1951?

The city seemed picturesque, perhaps a bit behind the times—it gave me a feeling of the day before yesterday. When I first walked through the streets I revelled in its atmosphere reminiscent of the 1940s, and I thought that it had an air of tranquility that was gone forever from cities in eastern Canada.

In that year British Columbia, with a land mass larger than the combined areas of Great Britain and France, had a population of just over one million people. Its largest city, Vancouver, could claim a population of 345,000. The Hotel Vancouver, the Sun Tower, and the Marine Building were the tallest buildings to be seen. There was no sign of new structures, no skeletal girders shooting skyward; there was no sound of jackhammers or the ringing of metal on metal to be heard. It was as if in their march towards the Pacific, freeways and subways and highrises and all the rest of the trappings of the post-war years had been checked at the barrier of the Rocky Mountains.

Within a very few days of my residency in British Columbia, however, I discovered that the province-wide atmosphere of tranquility in which I revelled was regarded as a smoke-and-shadow show by many of its citizens. Tranquility be damned, they said, it is nothing more than apathy and downright neglect on the part of the bunch of bums running the provincial government! Over in Victoria, the proper title for that so-called 'bunch of bums' was the Coalition Government. A union of Liberals and Conservatives, the Coalition forces seemed uneasy in the saddle after ten years in power, but were holding on for dear life. Such a coalition had seemed to make sense to the voters in 1941 when the Second World War was in full swing. Now, in 1951, the media, echoing the man in the street, reported that it had outlived its usefulness and was good for nothing except to cling grimly to power.

Critics of the government pointed to the highway system in the province, 22,500 miles of dirt and ruts, and to the provincial railway system known as the PGE (Pacific Great Eastern), eventually renamed the British Columbia Railway. This railway, said its detractors, started nowhere (Quesnel) and after several hundred miles of rail, ended nowhere (Squamish), adding little to the development of the province. Opponents of the Coalition positively frothed when they looked at the chaotic condition of the Hospital Insurance Service, with its hundreds of employees, its compulsory premiums which more often than not proved impossible to collect, and its chronic lack of hospital beds.

On November 2, 1951, oil had been discovered in the Peace River country. This was the first big oil discovery within the province's borders, and talk of a boom to surpass the Leduc oil find in Alberta was already sweeping through the northern half of the province. The Hart Highway, which was to woo the Peace River country away from Alberta and make it truly a part of British Columbia, was nearing completion. Meanwhile an oil pipeline was being built from the Alberta oilfields to the Pacific coast, work had begun on the multi-million dollar Aluminum Company of Canada's project at Kitimat, and the exploitation of the province's forests was about to swing into high gear with the issue of forest management licences covering 2.3 million acres of prime forest.

While the Liberals and Conservatives battled within the Coalition's house of cards, a movement soon to be led by William Andrew Cecil Bennett was quietly making headway among the electorate. Called the Social Credit League, it was sneaking up, not only on the almost catatonic Liberal/Conservative government, but also on the opposition CCF, forerunner of the NDP, which saw itself as the natural successor to the dying Coalition forces.

I was penniless when I reached Vancouver. The first few days were grey; fog and drizzle alternated to keep me off the streets and out of the market place. Finally after a week the sun came out and I plucked up the courage to do some job-hunting. For some reason one of the first applications I completed was for work as a typist with the provincial government—my typing was inaccurate but to compensate for that, I was swift on the keyboard. As I was about to leave the government office the receptionist said to me, "I see that you have had a few years in university. I think you should go across the street and see Miss Leigh. Would you like me to call her?" I had no idea who Miss Leigh was but I knew that I must find some kind of employment.

"Yes," I said. "Please call her."

Within moments I was in a building on the other side of Burrard Street. As I started down a long corridor I saw a woman, rather stocky and with a warm smile, coming to meet me.

"How long have you been interested in social work?" was her first question to me.

I was desperate for a job and the lie came easily. I assured her that I had always been interested in social work.

Thirty minutes later, after stipulating that there would have to be checks on my academic standing and references, and noting that I agreed to learn to drive a car and to take an intensive in-service course in social work, Amy Leigh, Assistant Director of the Social Welfare Branch, Department of Health and Welfare for British Columbia, launched me on my career as a social worker.

As Miss Leigh described the training program in more detail I was making a silent bargain with myself. I would take up this new career for a few months, a year, eighteen months at the most—just long enough to set my financial house in order. I had no idea then that social work would prove to be not just a job, but an addiction, with a pull that I could not resist.

The welfare system which hired me in November 1951 showed no signs of the apathy which gripped the government in Victoria. Far from a sense of lethargy, the Social Welfare Branch, part of the Department of Health and Welfare, exuded an air of achievement and progress and growth. This optimism was due in part to the fact that there had been almost a doubling of Branch social workers in the years following the end of the Second World War. There seemed every reason to believe that this pattern of growth in staff and services would continue in the years to come. We had, we thought, no place to go but up.

When I joined the Social Welfare Branch I found it rather like a club that extended across the province and which had fairly strict rules governing its membership—a sort of fraternity in which most of the members had attended university and everyone knew everyone else, at least by name. In that fraternity I was one of 160 social workers in the field, scattered in forty offices from Pouce Coupe in the north to New Westminster and Victoria in the south.

As I went first to the office in Haney and then for longer periods to the welfare offices in Salmon Arm and Vernon, I discovered that as a social worker in the Social Welfare Branch, I was involved in many different kinds of social services.

Across the province we spent much of our time dealing with money, or rather with people who lacked money. Social Assistance, Mothers' Allowance, Old Age Pensions, Blind Pensions—we took applications for these stipends, we followed up with regular reports on eligibility, we granted, turned down, increased, decreased or adjusted, the monthly grants for nearly 18,000 Social Assistance cases, 560 Mothers' Allowance cases, 32,600 Old Age Pensioners and 660 Blind Pensioners. Our grants, then as now, were not overly generous. Old age pension, for example, started at age seventy years and had recently been raised from $30 to $40 monthly. This could be augmented with a bonus of up to $10 per month, if the pensioner could show need and pass a means test.

We were active with pensioners in more areas than the financial one. We planned for them when their needs reached beyond the family circle. We arranged for aging men who needed minimum care to go to the Provincial Home in Kamloops. Regrettably there was no such service for elderly women. Once the elderly, men and women, became a bit addled, we sent them to Homes for the Aged in Terrace or on the grounds of the Essondale Mental Hospital near Vancouver. If the elderly were lucky enough to find an affordable private boarding home that would accept them when they could no longer care for themselves, a Social Welfare Branch worker was included in that planning too. We investigated boarding homes, as well as maternity homes, day care facilities, kindergartens, and summer camps, all of which required our approval in order to be licensed under the Welfare Institutions Licensing Act.

We were into the child welfare field in a big way: we took children from parents judged to be unfit, placed children in foster homes which we had theoretically previously investigated, returned other children to their natural parents, approved adoption homes and placed children for adoption. The Children of Unmarried Parents Act was a big thing in our professional lives—we assisted many a young unmarried mother to cope with her pregnancy through the use of maternity homes and, after the birth, with adoption services or foster care. It was always something of a challenge to go to court with an unmarried mother to establish the identity of the father of her child, known in the trade as the putative father. If the woman's action in court was successful, we encouraged the judge to order the man so named to pay up or go to jail.

There was more, much more, that kept us hopping. We provided innumerable reports and other services for a variety of agencies—the Child Guidance Clinic, the Girls and Boys Industrial Schools, the Division of Tuberculosis Control, the Division of Veneral Disease Control, the Provincial Mental Hospital, Crease Clinic—the list goes on and on. And, although the Second World War had been over for some years, there was more than one of its souvenirs left in the department—there was still a special section for Japanese indigents, and the Vancouver Children's Aid Society continued to care for a group known as Jewish Overseas children, thirty-four of them. Many of these children were survivors from Camp Belsen.

And of course, there were always Family Allowances.

Today the payment of Family Allowances has everything to do with proof and date of birth and nothing whatsoever to do with morality, lifestyle, or attendance at school. It was not always thus. In 1951, the payment of Family Allowances was automatic only as long as no complaints were received that children were neglected, unsupervised, or missing too many days of school. More than one school principal used the threat of a report to Family Allowances to enforce school attendance. For our part it was not uncommon for an enquiry to be made to our Branch by the federal government concerning the fitness of a home in receipt of Family Allowances. Often the field worker would be requested to administer the monthly five or ten or fifteen dollars when a home was judged to be improvident, immoral, disreputable, or disorderly. These were all terms used by Ottawa, and just as often by us, to define who should and who should not get their hands on this government bounty.

As field workers for the Social Welfare Branch, we had our finger on the pulse of British Columbia. And although in 1951 the pulse itself was sluggish, our touch was firm and steady.

We believed then that the Social Welfare Branch was destined for bigger and better things.

TWO

In 1952, a few months after my arrival in British Columbia, a provincial election was held in which the Liberal/Conservative coalition forces were decimated. Two things hastened their demise—the chaotic Hospital Insurance Service, which dominated every election speech, and the use of what was called the single transferrable ballot. This ballot, which the Coalition mistakenly believed would ensure its return to office for another term, allowed the voter to mark a first, second, third, and fourth choice of candidate.

As election day drew near, one heard more and more about a surging Social Credit movement. Men like Bert Price, Lyle Wicks, and Eric Martin, dedicated followers of Major Douglas' Social Credit theories, were heralding the need for change and, according to the media, voters were beginning to listen. Longtime Conservative William Andrew Cecil Bennett attended his first Social Credit meeting in 1951, and was immediately nominated as a Social Credit candidate; now, in 1952, he was running a vigorous campaign for the fledging movement. Suddenly, as election day loomed on the horizon, the possibility of a strong Social Credit showing did not seem as far-fetched as it had appeared to be a few weeks earlier.

As a newcomer I found it difficult to take the possibility of a

Social Credit victory seriously—in Alberta, yes, but surely not in a widespread and varied province such as British Columbia. During the Depression years in Saskatchewan, politics had been a favourite indoor sport in our village, and along with the democratic socialist philosophy of the CCF, I heard a great deal about Social Credit, funny money, Premier Aberhart and his brand of evangelical Christianity. This fundamentalist religion was far removed from the rather sterile Roman Catholicism in which I was raised. In later years, and especially during the Second World War, the Social Credit movement was branded racist, anti-semitic, anti-democratic, right-wing. This view of orthodox Social Credit gained some credence with me when I attended philosophy seminars conducted in the late 1940s by a professor at the University of Toronto, Dr. John Irving. He had completed an in-depth study of Social Credit as it functioned in Alberta and, like many others, he found racism and anti-semitism inherent in its social and political philosophy.

Nothing I had heard about orthodox Social Credit gave it credibility with me; I could not take it seriously, and could not believe that the masses of voters would find it any less acceptable than I did. As the election results rolled in, however, it became apparent that the voters of British Columbia were much less concerned with labels and political philosophies than me. One woman spoke for many when she told a reporter after the election: "I didn't know anything about Social Credit before the campaign, and I still don't. But I wanted to give a slap on the nose to the government!"

The counting of those strange transferrable ballots began June 12, the night of the election. First choice votes were counted and the chaotic results which had been predicted by many political pundits were announced the next day—the CCF had thirty percent of the vote, Social Credit had twenty-seven percent, and the balance of the popular vote was split between Liberal, Conservative, and old Coalition forces. Three weeks later, on July 3, the second, third, and fourth counts began. This painful procedure dragged on and for weeks it was impossible to tell whether Social Credit or the CCF would replace the moribund Coalition forces. When the fourth choice on the last ballot was finally counted, the Liberals and Conservatives had self-destructed and Social Credit, with nineteen seats compared to the CCF's eighteen, was called upon to form the government. Not until one month after election day was W.A.C. Bennett named the leader of Social Credit and soon after, premier of the province.

A second election a year later in June 1953 was the last time the single transferrable ballot was used in the province; in that election Social Credit gained twenty-eight seats, the CCF dropped to fourteen, and the remaining seats went to four Liberals, one Conservative, and one Independent.

After that second election, my friends and I asked each other, "Could the Social Credit be here to stay?"

As the weeks of my service in the Social Welfare Branch turned into months and then years, I began to realize that the British Columbia to which I had come in 1951 was changing almost beyond recognition.

The new premier, bringing his small business know-how from Kelowna to Victoria, was determined to run the government on the same free-enterprise principles which he had used so successfully to build his hardware empire in the Okanagan Valley. The government moved quickly to solve the Hospital Insurance chaos which had dominated previous sittings of the legislature—premiums were cancelled, to be replaced by an increase in sales tax from three percent to five percent, and the massive Health Insurance bureaucracy was disbanded. By 1954, the Pacific Great Eastern Railway was extended to Prince George. The next move, we were told, would be to put down track from Squamish to North Vancouver. When the first train rolled into Prince George, a cabinet minister leaped off the PGE shouting, "Prince George, Egad!" The Ministry of Public Works was to become the Department of Highways, with flamboyant Phil Gaglardi as its minister. We watched as the roads of the province were constructed, straightened, raised, lowered, bridged, re-routed, tunnelled, and paved, all under the manic direction of Flying Phil.

Although I had never regarded Social Credit as a government of social reform, I comforted myself after the elections of 1952 and 1953 with the belief that the welfare system was too firmly entrenched in the province to be destroyed. After all, Social Credit had this 'Onward-Christian-Soldiers' motif. Surely, I thought, one could depend on the new government to turn eventually from its obsession with road and rail to the needs of the elderly, the disadvantaged, and especially the children in the province.

I waited for that move. Like other social workers in the province, I had my shopping list ready: treatment centres for disturbed children and adults, increased money payments to the poor of all ages, programs for the rehabilitation of socially dysfunctional people, agreements between the federal and provincial governments to begin attacking the terrible conditions on Indian reservations, housing units for senior citizens—the list went on and on.

By the time I arrived in the Prince George welfare office in May

1954, I was thirty years old, single, and filled with a bounding energy just waiting to be lavished on my particular bailiwick. Along with that energy, however, there was also a growing disillusionment—I was beginning to realize that for this strange amalgam of politicians running things in Victoria, the 'Onward-Christian-Soldiers' motif might not necessarily include welfare recipients, and that if the obsession with road and rail continued long enough, our once proud social services system could be left in tatters.

The very area in central British Columbia in which I was expected to dispense social services reinforced this mounting disillusionment. Its size, its roads, its treacherous weather conditions all combined to ensure that the network of welfare services I could provide would be minimal at best.

Starting in Prince George, my region extended sixty miles across dirt roads to Vanderhoof located in the exact centre of the province. West of Vanderhoof I travelled fifty miles and more to the settlements of Fort Fraser, Fraser Lake, Endako, and beyond. I drove south from those settlements over logging roads to reach a number of homes. North from Vanderhoof, I covered the forty miles to Fort St. James, again on dirt roads, and to any settlement beyond there that could be reached by logging roads. In that huge wooded territory which I reckoned to be about the size of Holland, I was responsible for the elderly, children, the poor, people of all ages with mental and social problems, and the infirm. My area included one Indian residential school, Lejac, on Fraser Lake, and five Indian reservations, every one of them a textbook study in poverty, disease, and despair.

And the cars—nowhere was the determined penny-pinching of the government towards the welfare department more evident than in the area of government cars. Many years later I heard a rumour (which might well have been true) that when Premier Bennett received three requests for new cars, he randomly tore up two orders and granted the third!

A few months after my arrival in Prince George, I met a handsome charming Irishman named Pat Moran. I had first seen Pat in his uncle's hotel. I was there to make arrangements to drive one of the hotel's guests, an old-age pensioner, to his home near Vanderhoof. Pat was leaning on a counter and, with his back turned towards us, he was watching me in a large wall mirror when our eyes met.

Shortly after that first sighting, I accompanied some friends to a Sunday night March of Dimes dance. Soon after the music began Pat introduced himself. I learned later than an Irish RCMP officer on duty at the dance knew me slightly and when Pat arrived, informed him that inside the hall was an Irish girl named Bridget with red hair. As we danced Pat told me that he was born in County Mayo in Ireland, that he had come to Prince George in 1950 to work for his uncle, hotelman Paddy Moran, who was also city magistrate, and that his mother (who had died when he was three years old) and one of his sisters were also named Bridget. There was no time for him to say another word—our friend, the Irish RCMP officer, suddenly appeared, stopped the music, and announced that he had just received orders to close down the dance. In 1954, public dancing on Sundays was not allowed, even in the name of charity!

Pat and I weathered many storms in those first months—he was unsettled working in his uncle's hotel, I was on the road one week out of three, and we were both perennially short of ready cash. Still, we skated and went to movies, we played ping-pong and explored the countryside in his 1948 Chev, we drank hot rums with a trapper friend of Pat's in a forestry cabin, and every Saturday night we danced.

Before I quite realized what was happening, Pat had become a part of my life.

THREE

Despite my growing frustration in the field and a burgeoning romance on the homefront, the work went on.

It was an autumn morning in the mid-1950s, one of those glorious days in late September in central British Columbia when an early fog had been burned away by the sun, and now the leaves were golden in the sunlight. I was on my way to Vanderhoof and points west and north, and five days of intensive work.

My first stop was in a clearing forty-five miles west of Prince George. I ran the car into an opening in the woods just off the highway and hiked a barely discernible trail two miles into the bush to visit Mike, an old-age pensioner and something of a recluse. The day before I had sent a message over the local radio station to warn him of my visit. This service enabled social workers and public health nurses and a variety of other professionals to reach people who lived far beyond the ring of a telephone. Many of the individuals we served listened to the radio messages with all the enthusiasm of pioneers of another generation who had listened in on party lines.

Mike's dog was tied up—thank God, dogs were the bane of my existence—and for a half hour or more we put our heads together to complete the annual Field Service Report, without which his old-age pension would be suspended. That task out of the way, I settled down to a meal of sausages, potatoes, and onions, fried together on his old cook stove. Mike's coffee always tasted as if it had been brewing on the back of the stove for three days, but I didn't care; my walk through the bush had given me the appetite of a thresher and as I made a real meal of it, old Mike beamed over me.

Another cup of coffee and a cigarette and I accompanied Mike to the barn. He had a team of horses already harnessed and as he hitched them to a wagon, I climbed aboard and rode in style back to my car.

As I left him, I waved and said, "See you next year."

"Mebbe," he replied. Then wagon and horses and Mike were gone back into the forest and away from my sight for another year.

My visit with Mike had been leisurely but from now on the tempo of my week would accelerate. The coming days would follow a pattern I developed in May 1954 and followed for the next two years: two weeks in the Prince George welfare office and one week on the road.

My notebook was full of reminders of the people I had to see in the next four days in Vanderhoof, Fort St. James, Fort Fraser, Fraser Lake, and Endako.

There was an old-age pensioner, a woman, who was unhappy living with her son and his large family, and who had written to me that she wanted to go into an old people's home. I would call at her son's home and advise her that she was the wrong sex; B.C. had no old people's home for women unless and until they developed signs of advanced senility. For a man, yes, I would have been able to talk about the Provincial Home in Kamloops, but sadly there was no such resource for women.

I would have to look over the bank account of another old-age pensioner. A letter from a neighbour had accused him of paying less for rent than he had declared in his pension application. And I would have to see old Dave. Due to an error somewhere in the works he had received an extra cheque from the government to which he was not entitled and which he had hastened to use to fix the roof of his cabin. The government was demanding the return of this extra money, but as Dave had explained in letters without number over the past several months, he was strapped for money himself and, regrettably, could not send so much as a—'plug nickel' was, I think, the expression he used. Now I was being added to the scenario to see what I could do with Dave. I wasn't very hopeful. I knew Dave.

So many old-age pensioners! My notebook was filled with reminders to call at home after home to complete yearly reports or to take applications for pensions or to discuss money or health or living arrangements.

And there were adoptions, investigations to be started or completed or turned down. I looked forward to two of the more agreeable home visits in the next few days—I had twins to offer for adoption to a young Italian couple, and a three-year-old boy for a family that had been waiting for an older child for many months. Less happily, I had to make at least one visit to the Vanderhoof hospital to see a young girl who had decided to place her baby boy, just born, for adoption. That would be a night visit and I might be with the young mother for several hours. One day earlier, a phone call from a nun—it was a Catholic hospital—had warned me that the girl was very upset because she had not been allowed to see her baby at all. She was finding it hard to believe that the separation from her child would be easier for her if she did not see him.

Foster children—I would try and fail, I knew, to visit some of the many foster children in my area whom I, in theory, supervised. Two child welfare calls at least had to be made, both of which I dreaded. One was to the Stoney Creek Indian Reservation nine miles south of Vanderhoof, to investigate the alleged physical abuse of a child. If the abuse seemed certain I could offer no help except to remove the child from his home. Everything else on the reserve was in the hands of the Indian Agent. I dreaded the poverty and hopelessness there, and I despised the apathy that allowed such conditions to continue. Another visit to a rural home that was caring for self-destructive little Timmy was mandatory. Timmy was suddenly exhibiting some very odd sexual behaviours. What on earth was I to do with Timmy? His foster mother had other children and she was afraid to keep him in her home any longer. She and I knew that he should be in a treatment centre, but Christ, that was like asking for the moon.

Scattered throughout the pages of my notebook, I saw reminders to visit Social Assistance recipients, some of them elderly men or women nearly at the age to apply for Old Age Pension, many more of them families raising children on the bounty of Mother Welfare. At a moment's notice I could quote the Social Assistance rates listed on the back page of my notebook: $69.50 for a couple, $97.50 for a couple with two children, $125.50 for parents and four children. In the next four days I would use these rates to explain to tearful elderly people and harassed mothers that that was all there was in the kitty—my bosses said there wasn't any more. During these home visits I would try really valiantly not to think of my own childhood and of my Irish mother doing battle with the village council for the monthly stipend she had had to beg for herself and her five children. When I was in the field and required to enforce them, the welfare rates and pension payments left me awash in the past and memories of the privations in my childhood.

So much for what my notebook had in store for me during the next four and a half days. I looked at the spot in the woods where Mike and his team of horses had disappeared, then revved the motor of the old Ford and pointed it west, in the direction of Vanderhoof.

And finally, finally, after all the work, it was Friday evening and I was on my way home.

As I drove back to Prince George the people I had seen and the homes I had visited formed a kind of kaleidoscope on the dark road before me. I saw again the sad little girl who had given birth to a baby boy in the Vanderhoof hospital, only to relinquish him without ever seeing him, and wondered if she was to be another young woman who yearned for that child for the rest of her life. I wished that I could have referred her to a Women's Centre or a Mental Health facility where she might have gone for some healing therapy, but of course such a referral was out of the question—she would have had to travel over five hundred miles to Vancouver for such resources, and even then, in all likelihood her name would have been placed on a waiting list.

In the darkness I could see old Dave looking quizzically at me as we pondered together the relationship between the government coffers and his new roof. The thought of the faces of the Native women on the Stoney Creek Indian Reservation when they saw my government car drive on to their reserve shattered me—they were so poor, so haggard and all I could say to them was, "See the Indian Agent!" I knew the Indian Agent, and I knew that they might as well talk to the wind. Oh help, help, help! I thought as those faces flashed before me again. And Timmy—what was to become of Timmy?

I forced my mind away from those images and thought

instead of the Fort St. James Hotel, and Annie and Dan, the elderly couple who owned it. The thought seemed to ease my fatigue. That morning I had awakened to a gentle tap on the door of my room, and there was Dan with a cup of hot tea and a plate of bread and butter for me. Before he had quite closed the door behind him, I heard the crackle of wood burning in the great stove in the hallway downstairs. Always I had that lovely awakening in Fort St. James.

I was very tired. I had made dozens of home visits, driven roads that would challenge an Indianapolis 500 driver. I had fought off one dog with a mop and had had a glass of the sweetest wine ever made with the young Italian couple as we planned the trip they would make to see their twins.

The trouble was that like every other social worker in the province, I was struggling with a welfare system in which the caseloads were skyrocketing while the resources to deal with them were deteriorating.

FOUR

As the tempo of my life quickened, the moments for thinking about the people I visited, those brief periods in a whirlwind of work, usually came when I was driving from one town to another, one home to another. Then I could ponder the needs of a child or a parent or a pensioner.

Sometimes as I drove along the country roads I would plan, not exactly fraud, but what I preferred to call a manipulation of the regulations. Henry and his dilemma would enter my consciousness. He was just coming to the age when he would go off Social Assistance and receive old-age pension. Henry had informed me that there was a little cabin out of town which would be given to him free of charge if he moved it from its present location. He had been offered a site at the back of a friend's house in Vanderhoof where he could set up the cabin and live, he said, "as snug as a bug in a rug." Required, however, was the sum of $60 to pay for the cabin's removal.

Many times I had applied to my superiors for what was called Emergency Health Aid for a variety of projects, some of them not unlike Henry's and none of them involving a large amount of money, and every blasted time I had been turned down flat. Driving towards Vanderhoof and thinking about Henry's problem I asked myself, 'What if I don't cancel his Social Assistance on the month when he gets his first old-age pension cheque; he will then have an extra cheque which can pay for moving the cabin. I can simply say that I failed to cancel his social assistance and I don't think there's a damn thing, short of firing me, that the department can do about it!'

I'll do it, I thought, and then I will tell Henry that if he brags about his little windfall when he is having a glass of beer in the local pub, I'll murder him!

More than once I made a split-second decision during a home visit and then used a few minutes of driving as a breather to catch up with myself. One early afternoon, when I had been in the Prince George office for a year or more, I called in at a farm home to check on a little black girl named Essie. She had been brought to the welfare office by a neighbour who found her on her doorstep, badly beaten by her stepfather. She was placed in a home about which nothing was known, a not unusual occurrence—at the time, every available foster home was filled to capacity. I was worried about the placement and when I made my visit, three days after the little girl came into care, I discovered that there was good reason for my concern. Essie was huddled in the corner of a room furnished only with an ironing board and a wooden box. The woman of the house, lean and hard-faced, paid no attention to the child; instead, she said to me, "Look at the way that girl crouches—isn't she like a monkey?" and then attempted to share with me her theory that blacks were more closely related to apes than were white people. I interrupted her diatribe and said, "I want you to pack up Essie's belongings—I am moving her to another home and I'll be back for her in twenty minutes."

In the car, driving along to another home, I thought, 'Moving her, yes, but where?' In my head I flipped through names of approved foster parents, knowing that not one of them could squeeze Essie into their already-crowded home. I shrugged. If the worst happened, I decided, I would take her home with me, or one of my colleagues would take her in for a few days. One thing was certain—I couldn't wait to get back to Essie and remove her from that awful room and that dreadful woman!

So many individuals I plotted and planned for as I drove from one place to another. There was the mother of a severely handicapped boy, whose doctor told me she was destroying her health, and the well-being of her family, by keeping him at home when he should have been in an institution; but when I told him the only possible institution for the boy had a waiting list of over two hundred names, the doctor could only shake his head in dismay. There was the unmarried woman who had just had her fourth child and was refusing to take the child's father to court for maintenance; the Native woman living off the reserve who had just heard that her husband in a tuberculosis sanitorium had only days to live; the widow and her three children living on a monthly social assistance grant of $97.50 who would tell me when I called that there was never any money for food during the last week of every month—there was no end to the people and problems in my thoughts as, winter and summer, I drove the highways and roads and trails of central British Columbia.

And inevitably as I covered the hundreds of miles my mind turned from worrying about individual cases to a more general anxiety about the Social Welfare Branch itself. Our caseloads were growing in number; neglect of the elderly, the children, the poor, the mentally and emotionally sick was approaching a critical level. Could it be, I asked myself, that government policy, aided by apathy or ignorance on the part of the public, would continue, would in fact become still more frugal, more illiberal?

This fear for the future abated for a time in the mid-1950s

when a cabinet shuffle occurred. Health and Welfare became two separate departments. Eric Martin headed the Health portfolio and Wesley Black became our new minister. Hope was reborn; surely a new minister meant a renewal for the Branch.

Civil servants close to the seat of power in Victoria knew something that my colleagues and I came to understand only gradually—the British Columbia welfare system bore the personal stamp of Premier W.A.C. Bennett. Welfare ministers might come and go; it was Premier Bennett who was in control. As the Minister of Finance as well as Premier, Bennett was adamant that his government would not create a 'welfare state' nor would it subsidize the people he regarded as lazy or improvident, the ne'er-do-wells of society. The fact that these same people often had children did not appear to deter him—by his own admission, the presence of children complicated but did not change the problem. His biographers record that as a self-made man the premier believed that anyone could do what he had done. He was certain that the road from frame house to the Legislative Buildings in Victoria was a veritable freeway, open to all.

As I drove from one town to another in the mid- and late 1950s, I found myself with a new worry about a phenomenon that had just begun to appear on the social services horizon—unemployed employables. These were able-bodied men from all over Canada who were attracted to the province by newspaper reports of abundant work and high wages. When the work and the wages did not materialize, or when the employment ceased after a few weeks, these same able-bodied men and their families with them were thrown back on the welfare system. It was becoming evident in the Social Welfare Branch that the boom-and-bust cycles which went with the vaunted industrialization of the province left many families in dreadful circumstances.

Increasingly Socred politicians from Victoria who wandered into our offices were not willing to recognize the link between their ongoing industrialization and an upswing in unemployment and social problems. In answer to the many requests we made, as individuals and as members of the Association of Social Workers, for more staff and resources to deal with increased problems, we were told firmly to make do with what we had, to get on with the job and quit complaining—one cabinet minister suggested that I cease whining.

Years later, Ray Williston, one of the most powerful men in the Bennett cabinet, came close to apologizing for the harshness—he preferred to call the approach 'conservative'—of the Bennett era. "As a government we were far too conservative," he has been quoted as saying. "I honestly think that he [the Premier] was too conservative. He should have had a little more generous wage policy; he should have had a more generous social policy. I think we were wrong, when we had the money with which to carry out certain programmes that should have been carried out. This is particularly true of some welfare programs, certain treatment homes for the elderly citizens— several things of this kind we could well have paid for and didn't."

On paper, there was no doubt the B.C. welfare department had one of the best social programs in North America. Our policy manual outlined procedures with as much attention to detail as a painting by Michelangelo.

There was, for example, a section in the policy manual covering Family Service. This section authorized field workers to provide whatever services were necessary to prevent family breakdowns. Our aim, we were told, was to keep children with their natural parents, and to remove them from their homes only when their mental or physical well-being was threatened. If foster care became necessary, the policy manual had many pages outlining the requirements for becoming approved foster parents. Prospective foster parents would fill out an application form, complete with references, including a medical giving them a clean bill of health; in the fullness of time a social worker would investigate the home, visit the references and do the many things required to ensure that the home was able to provide good and loving care. Regular visits would be paid to the foster home once a child or children had been placed in it, and implicit in all this was an understanding that the worker would spend some time with the child/children in private.

In practice we had no resources that might conceivably have helped to keep families together, and children in their natural homes. We had no mental health facilities, no family support workers, no treatment centres of any kind. Such facilities as transition houses, detoxification centres, resources for treatment of drug or alcohol abuse, rehabilitative centres for disturbed children, programs to prevent sexual abuse or wife battering—these did not exist. The result was that when we discovered a child at risk in his own home, we had no recourse but to move him into a foster home. This often meant putting children in any home that would take them, whether or not that home had been approved or even investigated. It was sheer luck that so many of those homes, the Pierrots and the Clements and the Parks, among many others, provided the tender loving care prescribed by the policy manual.

Years later, a long-time social worker talked to me about what happened to youngsters under our care. He recognized that children were the big losers in the welfare system. He said to me, "Looking back now, there are almost none of the homes

I used for foster children that I would have used for my own
kids."

Policy aside, in our child welfare practices we took on respon-
sibilities for children that we could not possibly fulfill. Over and
over again we played Russian roulette with the lives of the
young. In the end, when we removed children from their own
homes and put them in foster homes about which we knew next
to nothing, no matter how we cloaked our actions in welfare
jargon, we were putting those children at risk.

By the end of my first half-decade as a social worker, I was
coming to believe that the welfare department which employed
me was the biggest contributor to child abuse in the province.

FIVE

On November 25, 1955, Vanderhoof became something more than the town to which I drove every third Monday to begin my work in the field. On that date, when the mercury dropped to 49.5 degrees below zero Fahrenheit, Pat Moran and I eloped. In the little office in Vanderhoof's provincial building where earlier in the week I had interviewed pensioners and foster parents, with my sister Eileen and Vanderhoof's doctor Ed McDonnell as witnesses, we were married by the Government Agent, Lyman Sands.

We intended to drive back to Prince George after the brief ceremony, phone up our friends and invite them to join us in celebrating our marriage. The phone call was never made— Lyman Sands and his wife asked us to drop around for a drink on our way out of town. That drink turned out to be a reception with streamers and punch, telegrams from my colleagues back in Prince George, and guests that included some of the friends I had made in Vanderhoof. The afternoon merged into evening and still the festivities went on—we didn't leave the Sands' home in Vanderhoof until nearly midnight.

Although there had been bitter cold and heavy snow during the first three weeks of November, the weather was the last thing on our minds as Pat revved up the motor and pointed the Chev in the direction of Prince George. We were several miles out of Vanderhoof when my sister remarked, "Isn't that a funny cracking sound the trees are making!" Pat and I exchanged glances— we knew that trees made that sound only under the very coldest of conditions. He turned on the car radio. Before long we heard a bulletin informing travellers that the temperature was 38 degrees below zero Fahrenheit and falling, and that moreover, all traffic had been warned off the Vanderhoof-Prince George highway due to an overflowing creek. We found a roadside coffee shop still open soon after we heard this weather report; over cups of coffee we decided to ignore all warnings and continue on to Prince George. We had driven through the rampaging creek earlier in the day and found it swift but non-threatening. We had plenty of gas and a reliable car, we assured each other, and we were already more than a third of the way home.

Within twelve miles of Prince George, we came to Mud River Hill, a steep curving incline with a garage blanketed in darkness at its foot. The Chev started the climb bravely enough, but near the top, it sputtered, coughed, and stopped.

It did not occur to us then that the Chev's clutch had given up the ghost. "Nothing to worry about," said Pat. "I'll just give it a bit more gas on the next try." He gave it a bit more gas on the next forty tries. "For the love of God, will you stop!" I roared. "You'll burn out the motor and then where will we be?" When he stepped out and sprinkled sand from a highways department box halfway up the hill, he shouted, "Will you shut your gob and keep your goddamned foot steady on the goddamned brake, or are you trying to kill me?" Meanwhile my sister sat as if turned to stone, trying not to pay the slightest attention to this bit of marital exchange.

In the end we sat at the bottom of Mud River Hill until a

farmer came along at eight o'clock in the morning and drove the three of us into Prince George. We didn't have the heart to tell him that he was witnessing the end of a honeymoon—in any event he probably wouldn't have believed us.

And thus began our marriage.

Housing of any kind in Prince George was in short supply and we considered ourselves lucky to be able to move into an old army building at the end of the business section on Third Avenue, one of the two main streets in Prince George. We lived in the back of this rented building; in the front there were two cubby holes which in 1955 passed for suites, and these were ours to sublet. Like many Second World War army structures, our building had ceilings fourteen feet high. The first winter there— we lived on Third Avenue for eighteen months—we managed to survive despite a primitive heating system, a two-lid garbage burner.

We were not able to lock our part of the building since the only bathroom available to the tenants in the front suites was in our living quarters. More than once we heard a noise in the night, and followed it through to the living room, only to discover one of the town's homeless (sometimes recognizable as one of my clients) sleeping on our chesterfield, under the impression that he had wandered into a snug hotel lobby. Unless the sleeper was a notorious reprobate, we left him to continue his nap undisturbed; in the morning we would find our guest gone and our living room none the worse for the overnight visit.

Thanks to this 'open door' policy Pat discovered early that he could expect the unexpected when he lived with a social worker.

We had been married one month and a day when, on Boxing Day 1955, I awoke to find a man in our bedroom, clutching a bundle and whispering to me, "Missus, you gotta help me." I recognized him as one of my regular clients, a single man living on Social Assistance.

"George," I said, "what in the hell are you doing in our bedroom?"

As he started to tell me the reason for his distress, the bundle in his arms squirmed and I saw that he was carrying a very young baby. Social workers tend to make snap decisions and I made one then. I knew that the only warm place in the building was in our bed. I reached for the baby, placed him beside a sleeping Pat, and shooed George into the living room so that I could make myself presentable. When I joined him he told me that two days before Christmas a young Native girl had asked him to look after her baby boy while she finished her shopping. Three days later she had not returned and George, desperate when he no longer had food or diapers, learned from some of his cronies where I lived. Finding the doors unlocked, he had made his way into our bedroom.

I sent George on his way and phoned one of our reliable foster mothers, Mrs. Clements, to arrange placement for the little tyke; she had never refused to take a needy child. I stoked up the garbage burner and returned to the bedroom, expecting my husband to ask some pointed questions about his bed partner. Instead I found man and baby in a deep sleep. Pat said afterwards that he had reached out to touch me and instead had found himself touching a lovely little Native baby. He said he took the only sensible course open to him—he decided to wait for explanations, snuggled the baby up to him, and went back to sleep.

By the time we were married Pat had left his uncle's employ and was working as a corrections officer in the new provincial jail on

Bridget at Point No Point, B.C. in 1956.

Bridget and Pat, posing in front of Pat's first car, in 1955.

Bridget and Pat, with newborn Mayo, in 1957.

Bridget and Pat, with Mayo and Roseanne, in 1961.

*Rose Anne Drugan, Bridget's
mother, in the late 1960s.*

*Bridget's children (L to R): Mayo,
Patrick, Roseanne, and Michael, at
the trailer court in Prince George in
1964.*

*Bridget at her typewriter in 1976,
when she was working as a freelance
reporter.*

the hill beyond Prince George's city centre. Before long there was a change in my employment too. In April 1956 I was promoted from Senior Social Worker to District Supervisor. I now had an area as large as the combined area of Holland and Belgium and I was travelling as much as ever. I supervised the Burns Lake office, 150 miles west of Prince George, and in the east my area extended to the Alberta border. With Pat on shift work at the jail and with me catching trains or covering my area in a dilapidated government car, we sometimes felt like two ships that passed in the night.

But it wasn't all work. Soon after we were married, at a cost of $800, we acquired a fully furnished one-room shack and forty acres just out of town on the cutbanks overlooking the Nechako River. This became our retreat. Summer and winter, despite hordes of mosquitoes or snow that was waist-deep, we used this property which we called The Ranch as our other living room. We still socialized and danced every weekend when Pat was not on shift, and in the days between, we amused ourselves by looking at properties for sale that we couldn't possibly afford to buy.

The other part of my existence, the social work front, was sometimes as fulfilling for me as my early married life. It was not always doom and gloom in the welfare office. We rescued many children from impossible home situations, facilitated the return of many more children to their natural parents, and placed lovely babies with happy adopting parents. The lives of count-less old-age pensioners and single mothers and people with disabilities were richer and more secure because of our interven-tion.

But while this was true, things could go terribly wrong,

especially in the child welfare field. We always had a sense that we were too dependent on luck, a feeling that catastrophe was waiting for us just around the corner.

And every so often in the years after my marriage, luck was not with us.

The winter following my appointment as supervisor was bitter with harsh temperatures and heavy snowfalls. The Prince George office was using every available foster home, approved or not, for the children who were coming into care. As was predictable, some of those children suffered.

During that rugged winter three little children from one family, aged three, four, and five, were placed in a home where there were already several natural and foster children, all of them young. The foster mother, Mrs. C, had accepted these additional children only under pressure from our office—we were desperate for foster homes and we begged her to give the placement a trial. When she took the three extra children the weather had been balmy enough, but as the days turned cold she found that she could not handle the endless bedwetting, the effort to wash and dry clothes, the noise and activity of so many children cooped up underfoot during the day. After a few weeks she finally gave up. She phoned the welfare office and asked the social worker to remove the three children we had recently placed with her.

The social worker had no alternative homes and was being run off her feet looking for placements for several other children who had just been taken from their parental homes. She kept in phone contact with the foster mother, but day after day went by and the three children were not removed.

Luckily for those children an older woman, a retired nurse who had previously been their foster mother for two years, took them for an outing and, because of some statements the children made, she examined their bodies. Reports varied. The nurse and her friend, another well-respected nurse, told the local paper, "The children have all been beaten to an extent that is difficult to imagine. They are covered with bruises." The regional director of our branch said, "There was some difference between our opinion of the injuries suffered by the children and the statements made elsewhere. The social worker involved did not consider the injuries as serious [as the former foster mother] and it is only fair to point out that her opinion has been substantiated by the doctor who first examined them after their plight became known." Mrs. C, the foster mother, said the bruises resulted from bumps and falls, one of the tumbles being a fall out of bed. Differences of opinion aside, the children did have bruises and they were speedily moved to a foster home in Burns Lake. The other foster children were removed as well and it was determined that Mr. and Mrs. C would not be used as foster parents by our branch again.

Now the question surfaced: should a charge of physical abuse be laid against the foster parents?

In my role as supervisor I questioned whether they should be charged since they had been pressured by a social worker into taking the children in the first place. As soon as she and her husband had realized they could not handle the situation, the foster mother had asked, unsuccessfully as it turned out, to have the children removed. It seemed to me to be shameful to place a couple in an impossible situation, ignore their pleas for help, and then haul them into court when they appeared to have handled things badly. If, however, a decision was reached to charge this couple, I believed that the department of which I was a supervisor should be charged with negligence as well. After all, we had taken over guardianship of the children, and implicit in that guardianship was a commitment to give them a protected and secure environment. I wrote a letter to the Superintendent of Child Welfare stating my position regarding charges both for the couple and our department, and as added insurance, I read the letter to Mr. and Mrs. C and to their lawyer.

I worked late on the night that a decision about charges was to be made. When I returned home Pat said to me, "There was a phone call for you from Victoria. Mr. and Mrs. C are going to be charged." The culpability of the department, he said, was not mentioned.

I burst into tears. "It isn't fair! It isn't fair!" I kept repeating. I was crying for those bruised little children and for the foster parents, and I was grieving as well for the illusions that I had had about my profession not so many years before.

Mr. and Mrs. C were charged in closed court under the Protection of Children's Act in that they, while guardians, "ill-treated three children under the age of five." My letter to the Superintendent of Child Welfare was read into the record. Mr. and Mrs. C were found guilty and received a modest monetary fine. The negligence of the department was not, of course, even considered.

SIX

If enough 'For Sale' signs are pursued, sooner or later a deal will be found that is too good to miss. So it was with us.

On the first day of May in 1957, after looking at hundreds of houses and businesses, we moved to a property our friends facetiously called Cannery Row, and which we eventually named Morans' Trailer Court, set on the banks of the Fraser River. And while the river and its banks were lovely, the court itself was a sight to behold—trailers of every description, sheds, shacks, bunkhouses, garages, and outdoor toilets were set in no discernible pattern on the ten lots we called ours. On his first morning as proprietor, Pat took a walk over 'the estate' as he called it, and ended his inspection by evicting half the tenants and threatening to throw two others into the river.

On the same day that we took over ownership of the trailer court, I resigned as District Supervisor of the Prince George welfare office and began maternity leave. One month later Mayo, the first of our four children, was born. I did not return to work until after the birth of our second daughter, Roseanne, born on January 1, 1959. This return to work was premature; after two months I was hospitalized for weeks with pneumonia. When I finally recovered and was back on the job I opted for part-time employment, three days a week. During the years that followed I sometimes had a caseload of unemployed employables and spent time on intake in the office. However, if a staff member left and was not replaced, something which happended almost routinely, I would find myself out in the field again, covering a full caseload as a part-time worker.

As time passed I discovered that the more my private life changed, the more the welfare department remained the same. Money was not forthcoming from Victoria, and social policy continued to reflect the premier's dictum: "We are against the establishment of a welfare state." Translated loosely, this meant minimum under-trained staff and as few resources as the system would allow.

Theoretically our department solved rather than created problems; theoretically too the quality of life was enhanced when a social worker entered the picture. In the spring of 1959, as happened so often in the welfare field, reality once again made a mockery of theory.

Our office received a complaint from a woman living in one of the suburbs of Prince George. She said that she lived near the home of a couple, Yvonne and Lawrence, and that she was hearing the persistent cries of a baby in their home. When a young social worker investigated, she found a ten-month-old baby boy, Albert, who weighed less than ten pounds. Doctors who examined the child said he was starving and on the brink of death.

The parents of the child were well known to the Prince George welfare office, at least on paper. They were two of the many people in our area who had been ghettoized as youngsters. Yvonne had had her first child when she was fifteen. At the time of the neighbour's complaint she was twenty-two years old and the mother of four children. Her husband Lawrence was eight years older and had a history of convictions for theft, breaking and entering, and armed robbery.

In 1988, while Lawrence was in jail serving a fairly lengthy term of incarceration, Yvonne gave birth to Albert. At the time of his birth she requested that the baby be placed for adoption because her husband was not the father. Albert was in foster care for a brief period but when Lawrence was released from jail, the couple decided to keep the little boy with them and he was returned to their care. Subsequent evidence seemed to indicate that the child had thrived until Lawrence was back in the home. Later in court Yvonne denied that her husband rejected the child; instead she said that he was unable to take nourishment.

As soon as Albert's condition was discovered, he was taken to the hospital and after several weeks of care, was placed in the foster home of Marian and Roy Pierott, where he flourished. Meanwhile, the parents were charged with negligence and failure to perform their duty. Their three other children, including four-year-old Anne Marie, were placed in another foster home.

Four months after these events I arrived in the welfare office one morning to be greeted by the news that little Anne Marie had been brought to the local hospital by the foster mother in a comatose condition during the night and that an examination of her body showed some bruising. The child died a few hours later. The foster mother, Mrs. T, was charged with murder. Now there were three people to be charged: Albert's parents, and Mrs. T, the foster mother.

Anne Marie's siblings were removed from the T home and placed with Mr. and Mrs. S. Mrs. T was lodged in Oakalla Prison awaiting trial. The new foster parents, Mr. and Mrs. S, were recognized by a relative of Lawrence and Yvonne's while attending Anne Marie's funeral. Fearing a disclosure of their guilty secret, Mrs. S contacted her social worker and confessed that she and Mr. S were not legally married. At that time our department did not recognize common-law relationships, the result being that Anne Marie's siblings were removed to yet another home. Before many weeks passed, traumatized by the admission that their relationship was common-law and the subsequent removal of the foster children from their care, the relationship that for many years had been so harmonious between Mr. and Mrs. S came to an end.

Meanwhile, during her preliminary hearing, the foster mother, Mrs. T, told the court that on the night Anne Marie died she heard a noise and found Anne Marie at the kitchen sink holding an open bottle of liquid detergent. Frightened that the child had consumed some of it—Anne Marie had a pattern of drinking anything and everything—she repeatedly asked the little girl to tell her if she had swallowed any. When the child would not answer, Mrs. T said she slapped her and Anne Marie fell, striking her head against a bench. The autopsy following her death showed traces of the detergent in the child's stomach. After fourteen people, including doctors and social workers, gave evidence, the charge of murder against Mrs. T was dropped.

Two weeks later, Anne Marie's parents were in court, charged with negligence in the care of Albert. They were found guilty of the charge but before sentence could be pronounced, the young mother was rushed to hospital where she gave birth to a fifth child. She returned to court in a wheelchair five days later to hear the judge pronounce sentence—one year in jail; her husband two years, less a day.

I kept track of the whereabouts of those involved in this case. Lawrence and Yvonne were eventually reunited with three of their remaining children once they were released from jail. Little Albert, a happy bouncing baby boy, was finally placed for adoption, and Mrs. S fled to the shelter of the southern U.S.

When the trauma of these events had passed, we played the game of 'what if?' in the welfare office. We knew that there was nothing to be gained by going back to the time when Lawrence and Yvonne were children in their respective ghettos, but we wondered, when Yvonne found herself with an unwanted pregnancy, alone and lonely with her husband in jail: what if she had had regular visits from a social worker instead of the cold comfort of the monthly welfare cheque dropped in the mail? What if there had been a women's centre to which she could have turned? What if her doctor could have referred her to a mental health facility? What if, in the jail system, there had been an active social service department? What if . . . ?

The fact was that there were none of these things. There was only a contingent of overworked, often semi-skilled workers, attempting to keep one step ahead of the tumbling dominos.

SEVEN

As my vision of a social worker's heaven dimmed and finally was no more, I knew that I was not alone in my disillusionment. When I talked to department heads in Victoria and to social workers scattered around the province, when I studied statistics in annual reports, I knew that my own area was not just a pocket of privation in an otherwise healthy provincial scene. The plight of the needy and the deprived in the central Cariboo formed a pattern which was repeated over and over again in every corner of British Columbia.

One department head who condemned the decline in provincial welfare services was Amy Leigh, Assistant Director of Welfare, the woman who had hired me in 1951. She was acknowledged to be an authority in the public welfare field, not only in British Columbia, but across North America as well. She cited 1955 as the year when welfare services began a serious backward slide in the province. Before that, British Columbia had the most progressive welfare program on this continent. "This was acknowledged," she said, "both in the United States and Canada and to no small extent in the United Kingdom." By the 1960s, she added, "we had deteriorated to such a point that it is difficult to know just where we stand now."

The City of Vancouver's welfare department's complaints

were loud and clear—its caseload had almost doubled without any increase in staff.

In Victoria, Dave Barrett, a defrocked social worker who eventually became Leader of the Official Opposition and later Premier, had his own statistical explanation for the sorry mess that the welfare system was fast becoming. He pointed out that in 1952 there was one social worker for every 5,100 people in the province; by 1963 there was one social worker for every 7,500 people. Comparing figures between 1952 and 1963, he said that the population of the province had increased forty percent, the number of children by sixty percent, and that while caseloads for social workers had increased by almost half again (the social allowance and child welfare fields showed the biggest climbs), staff had increased by only eight bodies in all. No one in the Legislature or outside its hallowed halls rose to contradict him.

As one welfare official put it, "We are so busy taking applications for aid that we actually give very little real help."

Ruby McKay, Superintendent of Child Welfare, was the first person in the department to publicly condemn government policies.

I first met her during an In-Service training session in February, 1952. In that session the trainees, male and female alike, fell in love with her within the first ten minutes of meeting her. She was about forty-five, and had silver hair and a face that was lovely to behold. In time we learned that that gentle façade concealed a will of iron, and that if there was ever a conflict between ourselves and a foster child, Ruby McKay would feed us to the lions without batting an eye. Her dedication to needy, abused, or neglected children was total, and over the years we were careful not to tangle with that dedication.

She often quoted the lines by which she lived:

He who gives a child a home
Builds palaces in Kingdom come.

When she resigned in December 1960 there was a sense of loss and disbelief in every corner of the province. Her resignation was quintessential Ruby McKay. As a good and loyal civil servant, she was determined to do the ethical thing—she resigned and only then did she make her reasons public. She could not, she said, work any longer with the "government's restrictive policies in the Child Welfare field."

The debate following her resignation was loud and prolonged. At one point in the dialogue the Honourable Phil Gaglardi, Minister of Highways, said that Miss McKay's charges were false and entirely political. The head of the B.C. Association of Social Workers was quick to reply that Mr. Gaglardi should have his mouth washed out with soft soap!

Paddy Sherman, reporting for the *Province* from its Victoria bureau in 1964, wrote: "After Miss McKay's resignation professional colleagues rallied around her. The Community Chest, the Parent-Teacher Federation, social workers, all demanded an inquiry and immediate improvement. There was no inquiry. The McKay affair fizzled."

Sadly, his words were true.

Through to 1963, the complaints from staff about welfare services continued. They were kept inside the department itself, but within that professional ethos they were bitter enough. At conferences, in inter-departmental memos, in long-distance calls, my colleagues and I and some of the top welfare officials warned that the neglect of the social services system could not continue. The power structure was repeatedly admonished that if it refused to pay now, it would pay later in the form of increased welfare rolls, and overcrowded jails, reform schools, and mental hospitals.

Premier Bennett, Highways Minister Gaglardi, Welfare Minister Wesley Black, Health Minister Eric Martin and other Social Credit MLAs shrugged off the concerns of social workers and parent-teacher groups, unions, churches, and any number of community organizations.

The policy of 'as little as possible, as slowly as possible' continued to bear Victoria's stamp of approval.

EIGHT

On Valentine's Day, 1962, I gave birth to our third child, Patrick, and four months later, in a pattern that was becoming familiar, I returned to my part-time work in the Prince George welfare office. Something else was very familiar—I was again covering a full caseload in my three days of employment each week.

During the fall of 1963, a Native woman, a widow with six children living on Social Assistance, asked for my help with her thirteen-year-old daughter who was a chronic runaway. The mother had been living in a remote area 150 miles from the nearest welfare office. She told me that when her worries with Winnie began, she had a great deal of help from relatives and a young RCMP officer, but the problem did not go away. Finally, in desperation, she moved with her children to Prince George, hoping that in what seemed a big city to her, she might find the help she needed.

She told me that Winnie had been a model child, quiet and dependable, until the death of her father in a car accident a few months before. Winnie had been very close to her father. After the father's death, the mother attempted to comfort her and help her with her grief. The child would not be comforted. Her reaction was to run away, to disappear for days at a time. Any attempt to talk to her, to tell her how dangerous her disappearances could be for her, met with stony silence. The mother had hoped that the move to a new environment might solve the problem, but instead the pattern of running away continued and in fact, grew more frequent. Very soon after the family arrived in Prince George, Winnie's mother brought her to my office and asked for my help.

Winnie was uncommunicative but from the very few words she uttered it was obvious that she hated everyone—herself, her mother, everyone with whom she had any contact. It seemed to me that she blamed everyone for continuing to live when her father was dead. She wasn't able to articulate the phrase, "It isn't fair!," but that sense of cosmic injustice was almost palpable. I knew from talking to her that this child was in a self-destructive pattern and that something had to be done about it.

Before I had a chance to see Winnie a second time, she disappeared for four days. In those four days her mother was in constant contact with me. Upon Winnie's return, mother and daughter came to my office, where Winnie said that she hated her home and the little kids in it and that she wanted to go into a foster home. The mother agreed to this with a feeling of relief. As she signed the consent forms for the department to look after her child, she said that it was true, there were too many kids at home and that Winnie might get more attention in a foster home.

I wasn't in the happy position of being able to go through a list of approved foster homes to find one that would meet Winnie's needs. In the entire Prince George area we had one vacancy for a teenager. A phone call confirmed that this foster home would take Winnie on a trial basis. I noticed that Winnie's body relaxed when this placement was confirmed; her relief was visible and I wondered if the pattern of disappearing that she had developed was beginning to frighten her, if perhaps she found that in the end it didn't help to run.

Four days later, just as I was about to eat the evening meal with my family, the phone rang. It was Winnie's foster mother and she was frantic. Winnie had been late coming home from school that afternoon, and she had scolded her. Before she could stop her, the foster mother said, Winnie had grabbed the object nearest to her hand, a bottle of ink, and had gulped it down before she could be stopped.

"Hold tight!" I said. "I'll be right there."

I was terrified as I drove to the foster home and from there, with a hysterical Winnie beside me, on to the hospital—was ink, I kept asking myself, lethal? What would I do if she had a seizure or died while I was driving?

We were a sight, the two of us, as we plunged through the doors of the Prince George Hospital's emergency room. I was in my usual off-duty disarray, and Winnie, ink and tears and mucous obscuring her features, stopped the entire staff in their tracks. That was one time when there was no waiting for attention in emergency.

As soon as the young doctor on duty established that Winnie had consumed ordinary blue ink, he hastened to assure everyone, staff included, that ink contained nothing which could be considered life-threatening. He smiled as he assured everyone that the only effect of Winnie's action would be that "her stool will be very dark for a day or two."

A nurse took Winnie away to clean her up.

The doctor wasn't smiling when he was alone with me. He said, "You are very lucky—that could as easily have been a bottle of bleach or some other lethal substance."

"I know! I know!"

"Of course this girl is very dangerous to herself," the doctor continued. "It seems to me that she needs psychiatric help . . . ."

That ended our discussion—we both knew that the help he was suggesting was non-existent.

I phoned the foster mother from the emergency ward to assure her that the ink had done no irreparable harm. When I said that I would be right back with Winnie, she interrupted me. She was really sorry, she said, but she didn't think she could handle Winnie any longer . . . she had to think of her own family and the two other foster girls in the home.

There was no choice but to return Winnie to her startled mother, with the warning to hide bleach, aspirins, and any other dangerous substance that might be in the home.

I didn't sleep very soundly that night.

When I visited Winnie's mother the next day, we discussed her daughter's need for help. I explained that the only hope of Winnie getting the psychiatric help she needed was for the mother to lay a charge of incorrigibility along with a request that Winnie be admitted to Willingdon School, the reform school for girls. I told her that there was no guarantee that the girl would get help even there—my information was that a psychiatrist visited the reform school for only a very few hours each month.

To criminalize the child, to send her to a reform school in the hope that she might get the psychiatric help she needed, seemed itself to be a criminal act. In the end Winnie's mother decided to give it one more try.

I returned Winnie to her mother on a Monday evening towards the end of December. On the following Friday morning, just as I was ready to heat up the old government car and head to work, the phone rang. It was the RCMP calling to advise me that Winnie was in cells and would be appearing in court later in the morning.

Within a few minutes I had the facts.

A few hours before, at 2 a.m., at the time the mercury stood at several degrees below zero, a resident walking home after a late shift at work had come upon Winnie stumbling through snowbanks in one of the city's suburbs, clad only in panties and brassiere. She was very drunk and kept talking about a group of men who had thrown her out of a car and into the snow. The woman called the police who picked her up and lodged her in a cell. Until she sobered up in the morning they could not identify her. When the police finally knew who she was, they phoned her mother who in turn advised them to call me.

I went to my office and from there I phoned Don Bingham, the Superintendent of Child Welfare in Victoria. I told him Winnie's story and asked, "In this whole bloody province is there not one home or centre where this child can be assessed and treated? Short of Willingdon School, is there nothing? For God's sake, Don, she's not a delinquent, she's just a mixed-up unhappy kid who's going to end up dead if we don't do something."

The answer was no . . . apart from a two-week assessment in Crease Clinic, always providing there was a bed available, and then—nothing! It would have helped if I could have vented my anger on Don, but that bit of relief was denied me. I knew him. I knew that his frustration, his sense of powerlessness, equalled my own.

In Juvenile Court that day, the magistrate George Stewart pressed me for an alternative to the reform school. I assured him that I had been on the phone to Victoria and that there was no foster home, no institution or clinic . . . nothing!

"This is terrible!" he said.

I looked at Winnie, a small sad figure in the courtroom, her body slack, her head sagging so that her face was barely visible through strands of hair.

I went further than that. "It's worse. It is sick, sick, sick!" I said bitterly.

I watched a hungover little Winnie being led out of the courtroom after she was sentenced to a term in the Willingdon Reform School for Girls. Something had tuned out inside me—I knew that whatever it took, whatever I had to do, I was never again going to be a party to the kind of thing that had gone on in court that day.

After thirteen years of compromise and making the best of things, that courtroom scene made a decision for me that I had been unable to make for myself.

NINE

The week after I appeared in court with Winnie, our Regional Administrator attended his monthly conference with the mandarins in Victoria. I followed him into his office on his return and put a few pointed questions to him.

Are any extra workers, I asked, being allocated to our office?

No, not to his knowledge, was the answer.

Was there any talk in Victoria, I continued, about setting up treatment centres or clinics for disturbed youngsters? Would the pitiful sixty-plus spaces in the province now available for treating disturbed children—would those few spaces be increased in the foreseeable future?

Again, the answer was no.

The day after I watched Winnie being escorted out of the courtroom, I had decided that I would write a letter to Premier Bennett and that in this letter Winnie would be cited as an example of the neglect into which our child welfare services had fallen. In order to rattle a few cages, copies of my letter would be sent to various newspapers and to the leaders of the opposition political parties. I composed this letter twenty times in my head in the days following my questioning the Regional Administrator. Finally, on a Sunday evening towards the end of December when my three children were bedded down for the night, I put pencil to paper.

"I could not face my clients for yet another year," I wrote, "without raising my voice to protest for them the service they are going to get from me. I have no excuse except desperation for what follows."

I wrote about the files waiting for me on my return to the welfare office after the Christmas holidays, and of the clients who, month after month, waited for me to visit them. "Some of the files labelled 'Visit—Urgent' have been sitting on my desk three or four months. I would not like to hazard a guess as to when I will be able to visit these clients. Each of them represents a problem, perhaps a serious financial problem, perhaps what may be called a social problem. A few represent problems that a psychiatrist, rather than a social worker, should assess. Many of the files cover mothers, widows, or deserted wives, who struggle to raise a family without the help of a husband or father. I daresay this stack of files on my desk waiting for me could involve as many as 150 people."

My letter pointed out that even if the staff were doubled throughout the province, we would still be in trouble. "Each time as January 1st approaches, I hopefully think that things will improve 'next year' and that somehow, in some way, I will be able to give better service to my clients. My hope has been frustrated. In fact each year my clients get service that seems to be just a little bit worse because as the caseload builds up, the demands for service exert ever-increasing pressure, but the staff does not grow proportionately. I find myself cutting a sorry figure indeed—a sort of frantic Peter rushing madly from hole to hole in the dike. The holes seem to grow in number but the extra fingers just aren't there."

I went on to tell the premier Winnie's story, ending with her appearance in court. "Once again, Mr. Premier, let me say to you that if this were an isolated case, I would not be writing to you. Every day, in fact, here and across the province, social workers are called upon to deal with seriously disturbed chldren. We have no psychiatrists, no specially-trained foster parents, no receiving or detention homes to aid us. We place children in homes that have never been properly investigated, we ignore serious neglect cases because we have no available homes. Inadequate? Yes. Dangerous? Yes. We need extra staff to find foster homes, to investigate them, we need receiving homes where children can be placed from court so that they can be assessed and the right home found for them. We need extra staff to work with parents in order to reunite them with their children. Above all we need badly and urgently mental health facilities at both the child and adult levels."

In conclusion, I wrote: "If we could ignore our disturbed children and adults in the knowledge that they would go away, fine and good. But, Mr. Premier, they don't go away. The jails and hospitals aren't big enough to hold them. The social allowance grants supporting members of dependent people spiral ever upwards. The group for whom I am begging help will continue to cost money, more and more money. So it becomes, does it not, a question not of whether we will spend money, but of how that money will be spent?"

A day or two before the end of 1963, I took my handwritten letter to a secretary in the department and asked if she could type it up for me without her boss seeing it. She glanced at the name of the person to whom it was directed and said, "I think so." I then asked if she could also make copies to send to the people on the attached list. She ran her eyes over the names: the Vancouver *Sun; the Province;* the Victoria *Daily Colonist;* the Prince George

Citizen; Robert Strachan, Leader of the Opposition; E. Davie Fulton, Leader of the Conservatives; Ray Perrault, Leader of the Liberals.

"Jesus!" she whispered.

On the evening of December 31, 1963, I dropped my letter to the premier, with copies to the politicians and the newspapers, into a mailbox on my way to a New Year's Eve shindig in the auditorium of the local Catholic church. I wasn't in much of a party mood. Reaction had set in almost as soon as the letters and I were separated. It is possible that for a few moments, if the postmaster had come to me and said that I could go back to the mailbox and recover my correspondence, I might have been tempted.

Throughout the evening, I reminded myself that a very few years before, Superintendent of Child Welfare Ruby McKay had done the ethical, the correct thing—she had tendered her resignation, made her public statement, and then disappeared into the limbo of discreet retirement. Let us see, I thought to myself, what this government will do with someone who refuses to be either ethical or discreet, someone who refuses to resign and who will fight like hell against dismissal. I took some comfort from the fact that in all likelihood my letter would be condensed into a few lines on the back pages of the newspapers and that would put the welfare farrago to sleep for another few years.

Throughout the night, as the music moved towards the crescendo of 'Auld Lang Syne' and with it, 1964, I told myself these things.

The solace that those thoughts gave me was questionable. After the ball was over and done it was another one of those times when sleep did not come easily.

TEN

The morning of Friday, January 3, 1964 . . . .

I was at the kitchen sink when the phone rang just after nine in the morning. The call was from a Vancouver *Sun* reporter who told me that the paper was featuring my letter on the front page of the Friday edition. He had already phoned the welfare department in Victoria to find out if I was some kind of a nut or crackpot. He had been assured, he said, that indeed I had many years of experience as a social worker, and he thought I might like to know that I was highly regarded within the department.

I filled him in with a few personal details, hung up the phone, and had barely made my way back to the kitchen sink when a strident ring from the telephone called me back. All day long, and the next, and the next, the calls came. There were requests for pictures, for interviews, for speeches to a variety of groups. Calls came from politicians, social workers, labour and church leaders, and many of my present and former clients.

Although we did not know it at the time, that first phone call on January 3 was a signal to Pat and me that our lives were about to change almost beyond recognition. During the first day or two we were surprised—perhaps 'stunned' is more accurate—at the reaction to my letter which came from so many quarters. If we had expected anything, it was that my letter would be quoted on page forty-eight of a late edition of the Vancouver *Sun*, and then it would be laid to rest beside Ruby McKay's 1960 resignation statement. Of course we had talked about the contents of my communication before I sent it off to the premier. In a rather vague way we had toyed with the idea that I might lose my job, but at no time did we look at each other and ask, "Should this letter be sent? Should it not be sent?" Far from such questioning, we were agreed that the time had come to alert the public to the seriousness of the welfare situation. Pat understood that I was no longer willing to be an apologist for government policies—this being so, any discussion about my action consisted of nothing more than a word here, a sentence there.

Days, even weeks, went by in 1964 before we came to realize that with my action, another dimension had been added to our lives—that along with my roles as wife, mother, and social worker, I was rapidly becoming some kind of as-yet-undefined public figure. But this was in the future. In the early days of January 1964, I reacted, responded, and explained, as the furor swirled around our home by the Fraser River.

Under the headline ANGRY CASE WORKER COMPLAINS . . . GROSS NEGLECT IN WELFARE CHARGED IN NOTE TO BENNETT . . . TRAGEDY OF DRUNKEN TROUBLED GIRL, 13, CITED, Paddy Sherman in the *Province* quoted much of my letter to the premier and then went on to write: "A social welfare department official here said that Mrs. Moran had been a satisfactory worker for years in Prince George but would not comment until the letter reached him. NDP Leader Strachan said only that he would raise the matter when the Legislature opens. The last time a government worker precipitated a battle in the Legislature on this subject was two years ago, when Ruby McKay resigned as superintendent of child welfare because of lack of facilities. She refused comment on the Moran letter." Her refusal was short-lived. Within two weeks Ruby McKay had dropped her self-imposed silence. Through the media she offered me her unqualified support.

In other newspapers my letter made similar headlines.

On the front page of the January 3 edition of the Vancouver *Sun*, under the headline FULL PROBE URGED ON SOCIAL WELFARE, a reporter wrote: "A social work expert today called for a public inquiry into the operation of social welfare in British Columbia. Prof. W.G. (Bill) Dixon, head of the University of British Columbia School of Social Work, said this is the only way to get at the root of trouble in the provincial welfare program. . . . Prof. Dixon said the last inquiry into welfare in B.C. was a private survey made in 1927. . . . All national statistics show B.C. is the province with the greatest incidence of social problems in Canada." The same Vancouver *Sun* reporter interviewed Welfare Minister Wesley Black and reported that the minister "agreed with Mrs. Moran that there is a critical shortage of staff in his department."

The Prince George *Citizen* devoted most of its front page to my letter and the charges of neglect that it contained. The Victoria *Daily Colonist* followed suit.

It was through the newspapers that I first learned I was not to be dismissed for my open letter to the premier. Minister of Welfare Wesley Black said to reporters, "No disciplinary action will be taken against Mrs. Moran. It is my understanding she is an excellent social worker and I have no derogatory remarks to make about her. The first I knew about her letter was what I read in the papers. I don't condone such complaints in the newspapers." He added, "I think it is unethical for people to do this sort of thing. She could have written to me, which she didn't do.

However, my understanding is she is an excellent worker and her services are very much needed."

I had missed the item in the news broadcast which placed Premier Bennett in Hawaii when I mailed my letter to him. The image of our premier lolling in the hot sand while a disturbed thirteen-year-old girl staggered drunk and half-naked through the snow was a study in contrasts which delighted editorial writers. One newspaper showed a picture of Premier Bennett smiling. "Premier Bennett is always smiling!" thundered the newspaper. "Smile at a drunken thirteen-year-old walking in the snow and desperately in need of psychiatric help!"

The inimitable cartoonist, Len Norris, pictured the premier strumming a guitar on the sands of Hawaii while a minion lowered a bottle into the ocean. Beside the premier a secretary was taking dictation. The caption of the cartoon read: "Dear Mrs. Moran, re your letter criticizing our provincial welfare program, I have immediately dispatched a directive to the department . . . ."

The original of that cartoon has a place of honour on my wall to this day.

ELEVEN

Since I learned through the newspapers that I had not been dismissed, and since no directive had come to me from the provincial government, I went to work as usual after the Christmas break. December had indeed been a prolific month for me—over the holidays I had learned that I was pregnant my with fourth child, due early September 1964.

I returned to work on January 8, and as I looked at my desk I was haunted by a familiar sense of frustration. As usual there was a stack of telephone messages from foster mothers, social assistance families, the probation officer, and, at the very top, a message to 'Please call' from Winnie's mother. On the corner of my desk were the files that I had known would be waiting for me when I returned after the Christmas holidays, all of them marked 'urgent'; many of them had been on my desk for weeks, even months. I pushed them away from me and looked up to see the stenographer standing in the doorway. "Bridget, would you please interview unemployed employables for an hour or two?" she asked. "The waiting room is packed with people who have appointments."

I knew there would be many more mornings which began in just this way. Despite the fact that the Cariboo was undergoing severe winter conditions, workers were flooding into our area from across Canada in a desperate bid for employment. As I began my first interview that morning—a fifty-year-old man from Nova Scotia who had come west in search of a labouring job—I found it hard to believe in the reality of my recent contact with politicians, reporters, and professional people.

The coffee break in mid-morning, however, restored my sense of the present; I was given a dozen or more letters and telegrams that had come in the daily mail drop. A pattern was established during that first morning which was followed in the days and weeks to come—coffee breaks became show-and-tell time as the staff and I read the correspondence in each day's mail. Although the letters, messages, and telegrams were directed to me, I became aware as time went on that a sense of common cause was developing, a feeling that I had spoken for the whole office and that the support flooding in was meant for everyone—secretaries, social workers, the supervisor, and, for a time at least, the regional administrator. Almost from the first there seemed nothing unilateral about my action—for six weeks all of us were involved and the responses to my action which poured in were meant for everyone as well.

Meanwhile, during the next few weeks, I led a kind of double life. During three days each week, except for show-and-tell interludes at coffee breaks, I was a welfare department employee, interviewing in the office, making home visits, preparing reports, appearing in court; when I was off duty, with each passing week I became more and more involved in my role as an advocate for an improved social welfare system.

The communications from the political leaders in Victoria— Robert Strachan, E. Davie Fulton, Ray Perrault, and Dave Barrett—struck a common note: they shared my concern about the welfare situation, they wrote, and they intended to demand a thorough investigation of the department when the legislature commenced on January 23.

Amy Leigh, who had hired me years before, cheered me on; she hoped, she wrote, that something would come of all the furor. "The government is so hard-boiled," she added, "and in the past has taken severe criticism on many subjects with a smile and a shrug of the shoulders. I hope the public will insist something be done this time."

I heard from dozens of professional people. College professors, psychiatrists, civil servants, and doctors, as well as various associations, societies, and schools of social work from across Canada made contact me with in one way or another. Letters and phone calls from social workers echoed my frustration with the practice of social work. Typical of the response was one young woman who wrote: "I share your sentiments entirely and in September 1963 resigned from the department because I felt I could no longer tolerate the situation. I was not confident enough to make an issue of it and feel that this is one of the problems that many (perhaps most) workers have. They are dissatisfied but don't have the guts to speak out."

Many clients and former clients contacted me. One of my old-age pensioners wrote: "While I am 96 years old, I sure agree this is one mess that needs clearing up." Foster children whom I had supervised ten and twelve years before wrote to say in effect: "I am one of thousands under the welfare system and I know your situation only too well." Workers with whom I had shared offices in a variety of towns got in touch with me—Lorraine, who had been one of my officers when I was in the navy and whom I met again in the Haney office when I was there in 1952; Janet, who, years before in Prince George, had tried valiantly, and unsuccessfully as it turned out, to bring charges of sexual abuse into court; and many other workers whose paths had crossed mine over the years.

In the more public field, the 'Letters to the Editor' section in British Columbia newspapers provided extra reading during our coffee breaks in January and February.

Most letters echoed our concern with the operation of the welfare department, but there was enough criticism of me and the people the writers called 'welfare bums' to keep the pot boiling.

'Taxpayer' wrote: "I say: thank God for Premier Bennett. If it were not for businessmen like him this province would go broke bending to the wishful dreams of idealistic sob-sisters. I felt as sorry as the next man for the thirteen-year-old girl described by Mrs. Moran, but I don't see why my tax dollars should do the job her mother wouldn't do."

Another 'Taxpayer' responded: "I'm sure the majority of fellow taxpayers share my view when I say 'Thank God such a cold-hearted, selfish, materialistic opinion is in the minority.' "

'Worried Canadian' recognized the welfare debacle, but she held Premier Bennett blameless: "I for one think it's very unfair of the people to blame Premier Bennett for the welfare situation. . . . Mr. Bennett was probably just as shocked and flabbergasted at the situation as the rest of the people of B.C. I'm ashamed to be a British Columbian after seeing how other people in other parties have taken advantage of this situation, but then some people never grow up. Let's start blaming ourselves a little and not pick on Premier Bennett."

Another writer felt that one solution to welfare problems was to exterminate the people considered to be 'unfit': "Why should citizens be taxed in order to prolong the miserable existence of physical or mental incurables, or for that matter, incurable hoodlums, incurable alcoholics? Let doctors forget their precious medical ethics and get on with it!"

Other opinions found their way into the public forum. One writer suggested that there should be a law prohibiting marriage under the age of eighteen for female and age twenty for males; another wrote that the manner in which I made my case was suggestive of motives other than the well-being of my cases; inevitably my ethics as a civil servant were questioned, and defended, in more than one letter.

I was much sought after as a public speaker in the weeks following my open letter to the premier. Whatever the setting, Parent-Teacher groups, the Mental Health Association, the Northern Interior Health Unit, the Kindergarten Association, the Prince George Labour Council, the Co-operative Society, I was determined to take advantage of the podium to detail the deterioration which had taken place in social services under the Social Credit government. What a sense of relief there was in speaking openly about concerns which for years had only been whispered about behind closed doors!

I spoke of the shortage of staff and resources in Prince George and stressed that these shortages were to be found in every part of the province. I quoted Roderick Haig-Brown, for twenty-five years a magistrate in Campbell River, an author of note, and an environmentalist long before it was in vogue. When questioned by a reporter about my concerns, he said: "Welfare problems are going to get worse . . . . The government takes the short view of the welfare problem. In my experience the importance of the welfare problem is always underrated. Remember, when we talk about one per-

son now, we end up with all his children in the next generation."
To give body to his statement, and to stress the fact that
society could pay now or pay later, but pay it surely must, I
described a study of a multiple-problem family group under-
taken after office hours by Don Kennedy when he was working
as a social wroerk in our office before he was called to the bar.
The study was updated more than once by other workers.
The statistics began in the 1940s with a couple I called
William and Nancy. They had grown up in the northern part of
the Prairies, had been disadvantaged as children, and were
illiterate. By the late 1940s, they had settled in what was then a
Prince George ghetto just outside the city core. Nancy had
fifteen children living; several others had died at birth. By 1960,
when the eldest child was forty and the youngest was seventeen,
all but four of them were illiterate. Thirteen were, or had been,
living on government funding; four of the males had served time
in jail; and many of the daughters were with men who had been
incarcerated for one reason or another.
By 1960, there were forty-eight grandchildren, which
brought the number in the family tree to sixty-five. Almost all of
them were being supported in one form or another by government funding. Many of Nancy and William's grandchildren
were in foster homes, some were before the courts on numerous
charges, and several of the grandchildren were already parenting
a new generation.
By the mid-sixties, Nancy and William's offspring had grown
to well over 100, and the pattern in the new generation was a
reflection of what had gone on before—at least eighty percent
were dependent on government funding; there was continuing
illiteracy, poor housing, and poor health, and a recurring pattern
of anti-social behaviour such as wife battery, gang rape, armed
robbery, drunken driving, and manslaughter.

When we worked on this particular family tree in 1963 and 1964, we tried and failed to estimate the money that had gone into the family constellation. We could calculate the Social Assistance costs, but it was impossible to assess the spiralling costs of chronic, long-term and mental health hospital bills, jails, courts, foster homes, health units, maternity homes, and transportation, to name only some of the services we considered. We knew that this multiple-problem family had cost many hundreds of thousands, perhaps millions of dollars—and there was no end in sight. The cost in terms of waste and suffering was beyond description and equally incalculable.

In talking about this family, I cast no stones at Nancy and William or at their many children, grandchildren, and great-grandchildren since, like the rest of us, Nancy and William and their offspring raised their children very much as they themselves were raised. I quoted the old Chinese proverb: "The fruit does not fall very far from the tree." Our welfare system, I said, guartanteed that the fruit would remain very close to the tree, since change was neither encouraged nor expected. The system, with its below-poverty-level grants and its lack of other services, virtually assured the continuance from one generation to another of poverty, illiteracy, inadequate housing, health problems, and dysfunctional social behaviour.

I pointed out that despite the premier's statement that he was against the establishment of a welfare state, the growth of hundreds of multiple-problem families like William and Nancy's across the province ensured that the very worst kind of welfare state was in fact being established in British Columbia. I always finished by repeating Roderick Haig-Brown's statement: "Remember, when we talk of one person now, we end up with all his children in the next generation."

Meanwhile, my husband Pat and my three children were almost as deeply involved as I was in what was beginning to be called the 'welfare controversy.' Pat was there to plot, plan, and to be the genial host as colleagues, friends, social assistance recipients, foster parents, and reporters gathered in the evenings and on weekends to plan the next move, the next speech. Often I would hear a noise in the night and find Pat in the kitchen, composing a letter to the editor of the local paper, or making notes to help me with the next day's activities. Our daughter, Mayo, age six, became proficient in picking up the phone before the third ring; a few seconds later, I would hear her clarion call: "Ma, it's about THAT LETTER again!" When Mayo was at school, Roseanne, age five, took over phone duty. She was registered in kindergarten, but trucked on home early each day because, she said, she had finished helping the teacher with 'the little kids.' Patrick was approaching three, and he was as unaware as a newborn lamb that chaos was swirling all about him.

During each of my pregnancies, I suffered for the full nine months with what I privately called 'pre-natal barfitis.' This fourth pregnancy was no different. I went to work and barfed, I made speeches and barfed, I answered the phone and barfed.

After a few weeks it had become a way of life.

TWELVE

A few days into January, 1964, the bonding that seemed to be happening din our welfare office in Prince George was put to the test. Regional Administrator Vern Dallamore received a call from Victoria suggesting that a senior official might pay us a visit, presumably to pour oil on troubled waters.

The staff in the office responded with one voice. "Such a visit is quite unnecessary," we advised Dallamore. "It would localize our problems, whereas we affirm that the deterioration in welfare services is province-wide in scope. Anyway, there is no sudden emergency up here—no, no, tell the senior official, whoever he might be, to stay where he is!"

When we learned that the official, Jimmy Sadler, Director of Social Welfare, was coming to our area whether we wanted him or not, we decided to present him with a brief. Signed by the social workers in the office, it outlined the same statistics that I had been quoting whenever I found someone who would listen to me. "Heretofore we have respected our professional responsibility and our loyalty to the Civil Service by observing the requirements of 'not talking,' " our brief to Jimmy Sadler concluded. "However, we feel that in any future speaking engagement, and there are several lined up, we will have to divulge present conditions. It has come to the point where each and every staff member has reached the point of no return, and we shall not return unless there is some indication that improvement is forthcoming."

Brave words, these!

One of the staff members tipped off the local paper that Sadler had arrived in town. When he was tracked down by a reporter upon his arrival, Sadler proved once again that he was a seasoned civil servant. He refused to comment on the "current welfare controversy." He described his visit as "just routine" and said that he was in Prince George following another routine visit he had made earlier in the week to the Peace River area. Sadler said he would not have anything to say following his talks with local staff.

Shortly thereafter, he met with us in the government building. As the meeting progressed, it became evident that he was not empowered to promise one single improvement.

"If you have nothing to say to us, why have you come?" asked one worker.

"I came up to see the situation for myself and to talk to you," he replied.

Our brief was presented to him and we went on to make certain demands—adequate office space, increased staff, and some indication at least that resources for treating adults and children were forthcoming. We requested a response by February 4, and suggested that if the answer was not positive, we would consider further action.

On January 24, one day after Sadler's visit, our regional administor told us that an announcement had just been made in Victoria. The Prince George situation was being rectified immediately, according to the bulletin. New offices were being rented to solve the problem of overcrowding and lack of privacy during client interviews; a mental health clinic was imminent;

and three additional staff members were to join us almost immediately.

As the days drifted into weeks we discovered that while rent money was available for new office quarters, the government was mysteriously bankrupt when the matter of erecting partitions was addressed. Two of the three new recruits who were to arrive 'immediately' never did arrive, and if they had, we were so short of space that we would have had to go on shifts. The mental health clinic, so loudly heralded in the bulletin, did not open until June, 1967, with a minimum of staff.

My colleagues in the Prince George welfare office in those early weeks were quick to defend me against any calumnies that came my way, especially if those insults came from the government.

Very soon after the Legislature opened at the end of January 1964, Ray Williston, our local Member of the Legislative Assembly as well as Minister of Forests, decided to give the legislature the benefit of his explanation of my unorthodox actions. "Mrs. Moran," he said, "was only a part-time social worker who became overwhelmed by her job." Yes, he went on, she did have cause to be disturbed, but the very things she was complaining about were being remedied at the time of her letter. "She made things harder for her fellow welfare workers in Prince George . . . and for the very dedicated group of civil servants who were moving toward the solution of this particular problem."

My fellow welfare workers in Prince George contacted the local paper immediately.

"Mr. Williston," they said, "is in no position to speak on our behalf. He was in Prince George at the time but he did not even put his nose in our office to find out if Bridget's charges were true. We doubt if he even knows where the welfare offices are located in the government building. If he felt any concern about the problem here he would have made it his business to find out about it when he visited the city in January. . . . Mr. Williston's remarks are just typical of a politician!"

THIRTEEN

In the midst of promises made and broken, and hopes reborn and dashed, the legislature began its spring sitting in Victoria on January 24, 1964.

This session held more than the usual interest for my colleagues and me; the leaders of the opposition parties—Fulton, Strachan, and Perrault—had written that they would be raising the issue of welfare when the House met.

Just over four months before I mailed my letter, Premier Bennett had called a snap election, and to optimists like myself it had seemed for a few halycon weeks that the government must fall and that a new regime would address the subject of welfare neglect. W.A.C. Bennett had been under much pressure in the late summer of 1963. The courts were throwing up roadblocks in his attempt to expropriate the private corporation, B.C. Electric, and turn it into the provincially-owned B.C. Hydro and Power Authority. At the time of the election call, no one could say who actually owned the hydro authority. As another part of the equation, the development of hydroelectric power was coming under increasing scrutiny. The Socred plan to develop both the Peace and the Columbia Rivers simultaneously, the so-called Two River policy, was criticized, not just by opposition parties in B.C., but by the federal government in Ottawa as well. A new challenge in the person of E. Davie Fulton, out of federal politics and now leader of the provincial Conservatives, had added another ingredient to the simmering political pot. Fulton had represented the federal riding of Kamloops for years. He decided that it would now be fitting for him to represent it provincially, despite the fact that Phil Gaglardi had long ago laid claim to this territory as his own.

It was a bitterly-fought electoral battle. Speculation ran high that this might be the election when, as one voter put it, "Bennett's going to get it in the eye!" There was talk of a possible minority government, formed either by the Socreds or by the New Democrats. With the Liberals running a strong campaign and the Conservatives apparently riding high on the strength of Fulton's presence, there were dire forecasts from the province's right wing that if the free enterprise vote were split three ways, the NDP might just have enough support to form a government.

Many considered publisher Ma Murray in Lillooet to be a harbinger of things to come. She had strayed from her earlier support of Premier Bennett. "Bennett is Public Enemy No. 1, and that's for damn sure!" she thundered during the 1963 campaign. "It will be a tragedy for this province if he is allowed back in for another four years!"

The campaign itself centered on the 'big' issues: hydroelectric power, the Two Rivers policy, big labour unions. Bennett called Fulton, whose B.C. roots went back several generations, an interloper. Fulton replied that Bennett, who was born in New Brunswick, was the real Johnny-come-lately on the provincial scene. In all of this there was barely a whisper about the rising numbers of welfare recipients in the province, the lack of housing for old-age pensioners, and the restrictive child welfare policies which had led to Ruby McKay's resignation. When the opposition politicians raised these issues, they were shouted down by what David Mitchell, Bennett's biographer, described as the "politics of grandeur" preached by the premier.

Newsman Paddy Sherman did not believe all the talk about a minority government coming out of the election. He had toured the province in August and September of 1963 and had found that for the first time, he was meeting people who openly and even proudly admitted that they voted Social Credit.

Paddy Sherman's instinct was unerring. When the votes were counted, Social Credit had increased its popular vote slightly, had gained an additional two seats at the expense of the NDP, and, perhaps most rewarding for the Socred faithful, E. Davie Fulton had been soundly trounced by Phil Gaglardi.

Small wonder then that on January 24, 1964, when the Legislature met, just four months after Bennett and his party had confounded their enemies at the polls, the Social Credit majority looked foward to a rather quiet few weeks as they went about the business of governing the province.

They did not foresee that the session would be a stormy one; equally unexpected for them was the fact that for once some of the tumult would centre around the welfare system.

Just four days into the new legislative session, the *Province* was reporting that the House was in an uproar. "The issue," said the report, "was a no-confidence motion by the NDP. It was made on the grounds that the Speech from the Throne didn't show the government was aware of the needs of social welfare and mental health."

Premier Bennett did not take this attack graciously. He used what were described as seven 'violent' minutes to tell the House that the people of the province had confidence in the government because they had re-elected Social Credit with an increased majority just four months earlier.

Liberal leader Ray Perrault was incensed by Bennett's speech. "We have seen an example of a pompous, petulant, predictable, arrogant, stuffy little diatribe by this premier this afternoon which does nothing to dignify this chamber and nothing to give an example to new members." Perrault declared that Bennett's speech had exhibited all his petty tyrannical properties.

Pat McGeer, one of Ray Perrault's fellow Liberals who within a few years was to be recycled into a Social Credit cabinet minister, had something to say about the provincial social welfare scene. He read excerpts from letters he had received from three social workers who claimed that B.C.'s welfare program, once the model for other agencies, had deteriorated into an understaffed and overworked service. He felt that my letter to the premier indicated that I was frustrated beyond endurance. "Mrs. Moran's letter focussed everyone's attention on welfare problems," he said, "because she is obviously not a malcontent, nor a person of narrow views."

This was hardly an auspicious beginning for the routine sitting to which the Socred members had looked forward when they converged on Victoria in January 1964.

FOURTEEN

Two weeks after the opening of the legislature on February 11, 1964, another salvo was fired into the 'welfare controversy,' and once again it travelled along a north-south path. It was to have a profound effect on my colleagues and me. Someone unknown to many of us made his own protest about welfare services and in the process turned my life completely around.

On February 11, Wallace (Wally) du Tumple, age twenty-three and a veteran of one year with the Department of Social Welfare in Fort St. John, went public with a bitter letter of resignation to Premier Bennett.

"My reasons for resigning have been accumulating since the first week of my employment," he wrote. "I am a social worker who has the Alaska Highway as his territory. My office is in Fort St. John and 1,100 miles of gravel road separates me from the remotest community for which I am responsible. The people I attempt to serve in addition to all the old-age pensioners in Fort St. John live in Wonowon, Fort Nelson, Lower Post, Cassiar, Telegraph Creek, and Atlin. From Mile 73 on the Alaska Highway, I am responsible for every facet of social welfare. In addition I am responsible for child welfare on every Indian reserve within this area."

Revealing that he had no training in social work and was not

in the least qualified to occupy the position he held, his letter
described his first day on the job. "Arriving in the Fort St. John
welfare office on a Monday, I began by counselling an unmarried mother (severely disturbed), two mixed-up juveniles, and a
middle-aged couple with marital problems. Quite a responsibility for a young-looking, inexperienced, unmarried, untrained
23-year-old."

Wally's letter went on to describe the problems he encoun-
tered in the far-flung communities he was expected to serve:
juvenile delinquency, alcoholism, child abuse, and child neglect,
a feast or famine kind of economy that fostered every kind of
instability. He described the community of Lower Post as the
most difficult of the communities, and one which he visited only
on an irregular basis. In that community of 150 people there had
been 132 court cases in one year. At the time that Wally wrote
his letter, there were seven juveniles on probation in Lower Post
and no probation officer. "No preventive work is being done in
Lower Post," he wrote, "nor is it being done in any community
north of Fort St. John."

The final straw for Wally concerned a child.

A small, emotionally disturbed boy who had been rejected
and physically beaten by his parents had been seen years before
on a consultative basis by a team of psychiatrists. They had
recommended intense psychotherapy in a controlled setting.
For seven years, the workers in Fort St. John had been trying to
get this child into a treatment centre. For seven years, the child's
admission to one of two possible treatment centres in the Lower
Mainland had been refused, presumably because of lack of space.

"Taking this particular case to heart," Wally continued, "I
wrote a total of six letters and as many memos. I received no
answer. At Christmas, I went to Victoria to see what was the
matter. I was told that a stenographer was 'just this minute

typing a letter to me.' " At the time of writing to the premier, Wally told reporters, the boy was still without treatment of any kind.

Wally ended his letter by saying that he had been tempted to resign quietly. He knew that would have been the easiest way out, and wondered if there had not already been too much publicity about the state of provincial welfare services. Then, he said, "I realized how the responsibility lay. I was burdened with a responsibility I could not shrug off—a responsibility to the distressed people of this area and this province. I am not seeking publicity for myself. I am seeking it for my cause."

When Wallace du Temple sent his letter of resignation to the premier, he set the date for his separation from the welfare department as June 12, four months hence. He said that in order to prevent disruption of the few services being provided in his area, he was prepared to work until a replacement was found. Then he dug into his pocket for $130 air fare and caught a plane to Victoria. He hoped, he told reporters, to talk to both the premier and the welfare minister.

Upon his arrival at the Legislative Building, Wally was handed a copy of the telegram that had been sent to him in Fort St. John, and which had not arrived by the time he was on his way to Victoria. The telegram read: "Re your public letter of resignation dated Feb 7 to Honourable Mr. Bennett. Your resignation is accepted as of today's date as a replacement is available. A salary adjustment is being worked out." It was signed by Jimmy Sadler, the Director of Social Welfare.

Undeterred by the walking papers he had just been handed, he went to Welfare Minister Wesley Black's office. There was no sign of Black. A stenographer told him that Black was giving dictation to his secretary, but that she would go in and see if an interview could be granted. "She was in there a long time," said Wally afterwards, "and when she came out she said the minister had to go to a conference."

Wally then went to the premier's office. He was told that Bennett was in conference and would not be available for a meeting. He waited for several hours before finally giving up for the day. He thought that he might try to see the premier the following day.

He made one other call before he left the hallowed halls of the legislature along which he had wandered all day, a briefcase in one hand, a looseleaf folder in the other. He called on Jimmy Sadler. As always, Jimmy was pleasant. During this brief exchange between the unemployed social worker and the consummate civil servant, Jimmy admitted that there were problems in the welfare field, but insisted they were being ironed out.

Some hours after Wally left the Legislative Building, a reporter cornered Premier Bennett in one of the building's interminable corridors.

"Will you grant an appointment to Mr. du Temple?" asked the reporter.

"No!" snapped the premier. "He's not an employee of this government."

Within a day of his arrival in Victoria, Wally was *persona non grata* to government members and civil servants alike. Now unemployed and with money becoming a problem, he had no choice but to fly back to the town, Fort St. John, which he had left so hurriedly a few days before.

He arrived back just in time to hear himself branded as 'young, green, and misinformed' by Jimmy Sadler at a Victoria press conference. Not satisfied that this had sufficiently destroyed du Temple's credibility, Sadler said that he had it on good authority—namely, from the mouth of the regional administrator himself—that Wally intended to leave the service anyway. According to Sadler, Wally had told the administrator that he wanted to return to university to study anthropology.

To add insult to injury, Wally's Fort St. John landlady apparently disapproved of his letter to the premier and his trip to Victoria. When he returned after his fruitless trip to the legislature, he found his belongings moved into the basement of the place he had called a home away from home, and two social workers who had been flown up to replace him were sleeping in his bedroom.

FIFTEEN

The week which began on the 10th of February was a time of stress for the social workers in Prince George. Unknown to me at the time, it represented something else—it was to be the last week I would work for the provincial government.

By February 11, Wally du Temple's letter was making headlines. Receiving almost as much press as the letter itself was Jimmy Sadler's statement that the Peace River social worker was misinformed. Pat and I sent a telegram to Wally, wishing him well. At the same time my fellow workers and I were approached by the news media from across the province for our comments on the du Temple charges. With one voice, we said that the government would do well to prepare itself for aftershocks; only a program aimed at massive reform, instituted immediately, would ensure that the Morans and the du Temples of the province returned to their proper tasks of giving service to the needy in their communities.

Sadler's statement left us with a bitter sense of betrayal. We knew of the years he had spent in the 1940s covering the central and northern areas of British Columbia as a social worker. He had experienced the vicious weather cycles, poor roads, and endless trips that were an integral part of a social worker's life in Prince George, Dawson Creek, Atlin, Lower Post, and the rest.

More than this he had visited the Peace River offices before he was in our office in January; Sadler was fully briefed on just how desperate the welfare needs were in northern British Columbia.

Late on the afternoon of February 13, one of my colleagues phoned and suggested that we send a wire to Jimmy Sadler stressing our support of Wally du Temple. We fiddled around with the wording and came up with the following: "As quoted in the Prince George *Citizen* of February 13, you have branded Wallace du Temple young, green, and misinformed. As social workers in Prince George we protest this treatment of a young social worker by a senior welfare official. It is no crime to be young in our department and we feel his analysis of caseload demands, distances he travels, etc. is correct. It is an established fact that many young staff members have aged prematurely on the job and we take our hat off to Mr. du Temple for protesting against this as he has done. We do not feel a senior official helps the cause of hard-working dedicated staff by using smear tactics."

"Should we make this statement public?" I asked my colleague.

"Absolutely!" was the answer. "Get in touch with the others and see if they want to support our statement."

By the time we had drafted our wire, the evening was upon us. I was able to contact three fellow workers—two others could not be reached—and add their names to the wire before we sent it off.

Ours was not the only response to Sadler's denigration of Wally. In the Legislature, Dave Barrett wondered aloud, "When was it decided that du Temple was young and green? After his letter? Was he young and green when he was hired, or did this happen to him afterwards?" Michael Wheeler, Assistant Professor with the School of Social Work at the University of

Front page of the January 3, 1964 edition of the Prince George Citizen.

Len Norris' 1964 cartoon satirizing Premier Bennett's holiday in Hawaii while the controversy over Bridget's letter grew. The description read: "Dear Mrs. Moran: re your letter criticizing our provincial welfare program, I have immediately dispatched a directive to the department . . ." (Vancouver Sun)

Bridget with the co-workers suspended with her in 1964. (Back row, L to R): Helen Gilmour, Shelagh Vickery, Bridget; Front row, L to R): Nick Proznick, Judy Kennedy. (Pete Miller/Prince George Citizen)

Bridget, with daughter Mayo, speaking to a Prince George Citizen reporter in 1964. (Pete Miller/Prince George Citizen)

"Trust Me": A Len Norris cartoon, published in 1972 after Bridget was thrown out of the B.C. Legislature in Victoria. (Vancouver Sun)

British Columbia, said, "Perhaps Mr. du Temple's real sin in the eyes of his employer was his refusal to accept as normal and inevitable standards of service which in his 'greenness' he knew to be morally indefensible and utterly wasteful of money and human beings." Professor Wheeler thought that du Temple's greenness was a positive virtue.

Two Socreds, Dan Campbell and Phil Gaglardi, both destined to head the welfare ministry in years to come, had a jaundiced view of social workers like du Temple and me. According to Dan Campbell, "Some teachers and social workers are just not willing to cope. I am satisfied that there are people out in the field who don't quit when the going gets tough." In the Legislature, Phil Gaglardi said that he thought Wally and I were mischievous and unprincipled. "I think," he said, "that it's about time we took a look at the moral status of the people we employ."

That evening, shortly after I sent off the wire to Jimmy Sadler, an enterprising reporter phoned me. He had, he said, received a request from Canadian Press for a seven hundred word story about the welfare situation in Prince George. He was looking for a strong lead line and since there was a rumour about that some of us were considering a trip to Victoria as yet another pressure move, he wondered if the possibility of such a trip might not be the strong lead line he needed. I said that such a trip had been discussed in a very nebulous way, that I had made up my mind to sit in the Legislature when the welfare budget was to be debated, and that other staff members had talked of joining me. I stressed that, apart from my own planned trip to the provincial capital, nothing of a definite nature was in the works. One of the workers who signed the telegram confirmed with the same reporter that yes, most of the staff were prepared to march on Victoria if that was the only way to get an improvement in conditions.

The next morning, I turned on the radio and tuned in the CBC. Imagine my shock to hear a report that Prince George social workers were marching to Victoria! The Vancouver *Sun*, the Victoria *Daily Colonist*, and the Victoria *Times* had blazing headlines announcing a threatened march.

That was another day when my phone didn't stop ringing. Newspapers, radio talk shows, and national networks phoned to find out more about the march: what was our route, how many social workers were joining us, and when would we arrive in Victoria? Hour after hour I repeated what I had said to the reporter the night before—I was going to Victoria when the welfare budget was to be debated later in the month, but no march was either planned or in progress. Foster parents, old-age pensioners, and more than one social assistance recipient phoned to offer help, and in the mail I received an anonymous gift of twenty dollars from a 'well-wisher' to help us with the expenses of the march.

Eventually word got through to the media that the march was a non-event and the reporters stopped phoning. The last call I had that evening was from a friendly civil servant in Victoria—I couldn't decide afterwards whether his news was good or bad. He told me that the blazing headlines about a march, on top of our public telegram to Sadler, had really set the cat among the pigeons in welfare officialdom.

That day, Friday, was a regular day off for me. I missed the meeting called by our regional administrator, Vern Dallamore. When the social workers were assembled in his office, he said, "I have had instructions from Victoria that your romance with the press is to cease at once. Any infraction will result in suspension." Although I was informed by phone about this cease-and-desist order, I went ahead with two meetings I had already scheduled for the weekend—one a private discussion with a group of foster parents, and the other a more public meeting with the Prince George Labour Council.

When I arrived in the office on Monday morning, I found the staff whispering that the Assistant Director of Welfare, Robert Burnham, had arrived in Prince George and that he was presently conferring with Vern Dallamore. There was some speculation: why was he here? Of far more interest to me was the fact that two new workers, Tom and Peter, had suddenly appeared in our office. Were we to finally get some of the help we had been promised the month before?

At noon the secretary appeared at my door.

"Bridget," she said, "you and the four workers who signed the telegram to Jimmy Sadler are to go upstairs immediately for a meeting with Mr. Burnham."

I wasn't unduly concerned. I had first met Bob years before when I was stationed in Salmon Arm and he worked out of the Kamloops office. We had suffered through many meetings together and had socialized on more than one occasion afterwards. I had very friendly feelings towards Bob.

As soon as our little group sat down across the table from Bob and Vern, I realized that there was nothing friendly in Bob's look as we exchanged greetings. There was no small talk, no comradely give-and-take. Instead, Bob immediately handed copies of a letter to us: "It is with regret that I find it necessary to advise you that you have been suspended, pending further investigation, from your duties as a social worker attached to the Department of Social Welfare, Prince George, effective immediately.

I believe you are fully aware of the reasons why this suspension has been necessary and it therefore is not my intention to set out these reasons herein." The letter was signed R.J. Burnham, for E.R. Rickinson, Deputy Minister, Department of Social Welfare.

Following a period of silence while we read our letters of suspension, Bob told us that we were to proceed to our offices, pick up our personal belongings, and leave the welfare premises forthwith. At the moment when he issued our marching orders, it did not occur to me that these orders completely separated me from my office and my caseload. That realization came a few minutes later.

"What do you propose to do about replacements?" I asked.

"We anticipate some difficulties," he replied, "but replacements will be here." He would meet with each of us individually, he said, to discuss conditions for reinstatement.

He stood, indicating that the meeting was over.

In stunned silence we filed down the stairs and into our offices, where we collected coats, boots, and purses. Before we quite knew what had happened, we were out on the snow-covered street, staring at each other.

At the same time that we were suspended, a sixth worker, Eileen Temperley, also vacated the welfare office. Her husband was awaiting a move to Ottawa and she had had her letter of intent to resign in the regional administrator's hands for weeks. Unaware that five of her colleagues were about to be suspended, she decided during the morning that this was as good a day as any to resign. Peter and Tom, the newly-arrived workers with half a day's experience under their belts, were suddenly the senior, and only, workers in the office.

❖

As we gathered on the street, I knew that the sense of surprise I felt would be less than the shock felt by my co-workers, Judy Kennedy, Nick Proznick, Shelagh Vickery, and Helen Gilmour. Deep down I had always known that inside agitators do not stay inside forever; sooner or later they are neutralized by the powers that be. It was otherwise with my colleagues. They had watched me attack the government with impunity; in some sense they had come to believe that I was immune from retaliatory action, and that this immunity extended beyond me to them.

As we stood talking in the bitter north wind, I made a discovery that completely unnerved me—I found that although over the weeks I had paid lip service to the possibility of losing my job, when the moment came I was no more prepared for it than were my fellow workers. For thirteen years I had been part of a team; I had had whole sections of one community or another in which I looked after hundreds of people. Now those same people, the foster children, single mothers, babies I had placed for adoption, and the many doctors and teachers and lawyers I had worked with over the years—at a word from Victoria they passed out of my orbit. Suddenly it was as if I belonged nowhere, that I had been cut adrift from what had been my world and was my world no longer.

Finally the chill on the street outside the government building penetrated our collective state of shock. A move of some kind became imperative. Deciding that courage of the liquid sort was required, we picked up bottles of benedictine and brandy at the local liquor store and repaired to Judy Kennedy's home. By the time her husband arrived for a belated lunch, he was surprised to find a group of social workers, unemployed, inclined to hysteria, and after two drinks, not completely sober.

Shortly after one o'clock in the afternoon, I arrived home at the trailer court to find my six-year-old daughter Mayo covered in spots. She had been sent home from school with measles. This outbreak of measles, I found, had a very sobering effect on me. Anticipating that Roseanne and Patrick would soon follow suit—in this I was not disappointed—I arranged with our doctor for a massive jar of antibiotics. Not only did the mild measles hit all three of the kids; as soon as they were over one strain of measles, they all broke out in spots again. The German measles had struck.

In a bizarre way, the measles, for a few hours at least, allowed me to ignore the events of that morning. In looking after my sick daughter and preparing for the onslaught of illness which I was sure was coming for the other two, I was able to put all thoughts, plans, and decisions about my suspension temporarily on hold.

SIXTEEN

On the morning of February 17, when I had asked Bob Burnham about replacements for those of us who were suspended, he had replied that, difficult though it might be, replacements would be in place. He failed to tell us that workers were already on their way to Prince George from offices in Trail, Haney, and Kamloops. My replacement was a district supervisor from the Lower Mainland who, I'm sure, had some regrets that he had written to me a few weeks earlier to say he "admired my courage, spunk, and guts," and wished there was some way in which he could support me. Fortunately his way of showing support was not reflected in the public and political actions which came from all sides after our suspension.

Three local women, two of them foster parents, Mary Hogan, Rita Tomlison, and Pearl Burgess, collected over 200 names in a few short hours for a telegram sent to Minister of Social Welfare Wesley Black. The telegram protested our suspension and described the welfare situation as 'grossly inadequate.' Mary Hogan told reporters that a sixteen-year-old former ward of hers had called her in tears after she heard of Shelagh Vickery's suspension. The girl threatened to run away because, according to Mary, "the one person she had learned to trust and respect" would no longer be able to help.

During its weekly meeting following our suspension, Prince George City Council called for a full investigation and report into the welfare situation in Prince George. Alderman Charlie Graham said, "Rather than be condemned, these workers should be recognized as having done a public service." Alderman Dick Yardley commended me: "She did an excellent job. She germinated a tremendous revolt in B.C." Alderman Enemark noted that the city paid ten percent of the cost of welfare and this being so, wanted "an investigation of the cause of all this friction in the administration here and the adverse publicity the city is getting . . . it's in our interest to know what's going on."

In the larger arena of Victoria, shouts of "Crisis in welfare!" rang across the floor of the legislature on the day that our suspensions became known. The NDP and the Liberals tried and failed to force an emergency debate on welfare. The legislators voted along party lines and the motion was defeated, thirty-one to seventeen. Calls for the resignation of Wesley Black as welfare minister elicited the information that he spent only two days a week on his welfare portfolio. He admitted grudgingly that the three remaining days of each week were taken up with the ministries of the Provincial Secretary and Municipal Affairs. He confessed that he had never been to the School of Social Work at the University of British Columbia, but hastened to add, "they have been to see me." Debate forced an admission from the government that the House Committee on Welfare had not met in over four years. "Neglect!" shouted the Opposition.

Reporters roaming the corridors of the legislature came upon Dave Barrett, who charged that the Prince George suspensions were "a direct attempt to demand conformity in the civil service." Another reporter, spotting Premier Bennett, asked for a comment about the turn of events in Prince George. "That would be an administrative problem," snapped the premier. "I know nothing about it."

Quite by chance, on the day that we were suspended, representatives from the B.C. Association of Social Workers were in Victoria presenting a brief to Wesley Black. The brief pinpointed the very problems we had stated and restated in Prince George, and went on to confirm that in order to meet the government's own standards (forty-five cases involving children per social worker), the welfare department required an additional 106 workers. The Association's brief also called for a twenty-three percent wage boost for social workers, increased treatment facilities and services for children, and a request that all levels of government get together to devise "an enlightened overall plan for public welfare."

Neither Mr. Black nor his office commented on the brief.

Letters on the subject received by newspapers in Vancouver, Victoria, and Prince George proved so numerous that whole pages were devoted to them. They ranged from comments by social workers who had experienced the same frustrations as Wally du Temple, to those scolding Phil Gaglardi for calling du Temple and me unprincipled. Someone signed 'Disgusted' felt that this issue was "being used by the political parties who are not in power, just to create a disturbance," while 'On Aid' wrote, "As a welfare recipient in poor health, I feel it is ludicrous to pay people more and more to teach people like us to live on less."

The weekly Prince George *Progress* carried a cartoon of a welfare line-up that included the five of us who were suspended. The editorial accompanying it commended the government for finally doing something about our treachery.

Meanwhile, Bob Burnham was moving through the government

building in Prince George in a shroud of secrecy, refusing to speak to reporters or to have his photo taken. Despite this, an enterprising photographer caught him leaving the welfare office and by the next day a large picture of him looking stern and determined graced the front page of the Prince George *Citizen*. Bob was heard to wonder aloud if there was a spy in the welfare office who had alerted the *Citizen* photographer. He and the regional administrator went on to ponder the possibility that the office phones were tapped. The secretaries phoned me from their homes in the evening to report that the level of paranoia in the office was beyond belief.

When we were handed our suspension notices, Burnham said that he would meet with us one by one to discuss the conditions for reinstatement. By the next day, when I suggested to some of my comrades in adversity that we should go to any interview as a group, I was a bit nonplussed to find that three of my colleagues wanted only to get back to work. When I thought about it seriously, I realized that Helen Gilmour and Shelagh Vickery were relatively new to the welfare game. Early on, I learned that they were under intense pressure at home to agree to any conditions set out by the ministry that would allow their return to work. It was different with both Judy Kennedy and myself. Judy's husband had worked for the welfare department before he began practicing law, and while there had had a caseload of 1,200 unemployed employables; he recognized at first hand, as Helen and Shelagh's husbands could not, the validity of our grievances. As for Pat, he had been an integral part of my life as a social worker for ten years. He had lived with my tears, depression, and anger as I struggled to bring some semblance of humanity into an increasingly unmanageable caseload. It required no words from either of us for me to expect his support and for him to give it.

I watched the crumbling of what just days before had appeared to be a solid front of dedicated and determined social workers, and wondered about the office bonding that had seemed so real a few weeks earlier. Was I to be left to swing alone? And then I remembered my New Year's resolution when I mailed the letter to the premier: under no circumstances would I resign, and if the ministry tried to fire me, I would resist. Let the others follow their own inclinations; I would be goddamned if I was going to give in to Bob Burnham, or Wesley Black, or the premier himself!

My resolution faced its first test two days after our suspension when I met with Bob Burnham. We had no difficulty, he and I, at arriving at a truce on the matter of the public wire to Jimmy Sadler. He saw it as an act of insubordination, while I viewed it as bad strategy. By then I knew that while the government might be attacked with impunity, it was quite another thing to take on a seasoned civil servant such as Jimmy Sadler. As Bob talked about the evils of insubordination, I nodded my head, thinking, insubordination be damned, what we did was just plain poor tactics! Our wire to Sadler took the heat off the government—it let them off the hook.

Bob went on to ask me for a solemn commitment that, if I were reinstated, I would never speak on the subject of welfare outside of departmental channels again; if I had a public statement to make, I must resign first.

"That is a promise I can't possibly make," I said. "I lack enough faith in the ministry to muzzle myself in the way that you are suggesting."

"Then," Burnham said, "I am prepared to recommend your dismissal. On the basis of the wire to Jimmy Sadler you are as eligible as the rest for reinstatement. However, your refusal to go through regular channels is another matter."

Two days after this interview, I was advised that the four social workers suspended with me had been asked to return to work on February 24. Whatever commitment Burnham had been able to extract from three of the workers ensured their return to work; however, he did not receive the response he wanted when he interviewed Judy Kennedy. Asked for a promise that she would not talk to the press about welfare matters in the future, she replied, "It would depend on whether I had anything to say. If I have something to say, I will talk to the press." In fact, one day later a reporter from the *Sun* called her and she gave him a statement about the current welfare situation.

Imagine her surprise an evening or two later when she heard that Burnham reported to welfare staff that all suspended workers with the exception of myself had promised to stop their flirtation with the press. Early the next morning, Judy and her lawyer husband tracked Bob Burnham down at his hotel. Judy repeated her earlier statement to him. Burnham insisted that he had a commitment from her, and that as far as he was concerned, that was the end of the matter. Obviously he had his weapons sighted on a different and, to him, more dangerous target.

As news of the reinstatement of the four workers hit the press, I was advised privately that in my case no decision had been reached.

The following week I had my second and, as it turned out, last interview with the Department of Social Welfare.

I met Bob Burnham and regional administrator Vern Dallamore in a local hotel room. The two men were stationed on one side of the bed. I sat across from them. Bob carried the conversation; I assumed that Vern, who did not speak during the two hours of the interview, was there on behalf of the ministry to act as a witness to the proceedings. Obviously, he was no longer part of my support system.

During this last interview, there was no discussion of the public wire to Jimmy Sadler. Instead, we battled over the ethics of the situation—the matter which Bob described as the integrity of the civil service and the deeper issue of what I referred to as individual responsibility.

Bob's position was clear. "The civil service can only be independent if it does not interfere with the government," he repeated over and over. "If the Civil Service has the right to interfere in government matters, the government in turn can dabble in civil service matters. In critizing the government, while still a civil servant, you have threatened the independence and the integrity of the Civil Service Commission itself."

"I can agree in principle," I replied, "although you and I know that the government interferes with the civil service in a whole variety of ways. But beyond that, what happens when the government is failing the people and only the civil servant has a detailed knowledge of that failure? Is it subversion or is it instead a moral, an ethical duty, to inform the community about what is happening?"

"Never! Never!" Burnham said. "A civil servant, while a civil servant, never, never, never speaks outside government channels!"

"Well," I said, "let's try it this way—did my protest do any good?"

"Yes," he replied, "quite a lot of good, really."

"Well, then . . . ."

"Even so," he insisted, "you should not have made that protest while employed by the government. You should have resigned first."

Faced with my intransigence, he became accusatory. "You

are putting us in an impossible position. You want us to fire you!"

"Bull!" I said. "I want more than anything else to go back to work. Reinstate me and if I do something the ministry doesn't like, then fire me."

"I can't reinstate you on those terms, knowing that in a day or two, a month or two, you might try some more tricks. I repeat, you are putting us in an impossible situation!"

We played this routine over and over again in the two hours we were in that hotel room.

It ended in a deadlock.

In the end I was hung out to dry, or as the official announcement put it, I was to be given time to reconsider my position. Meanwhile I remained under suspension.

SEVENTEEN

I had long planned to sit in the gallery of the legislature during the debate of the welfare department's budget and the minister's salary. When a reporter phoned on March 18, 1964, to warn me that this debate would take place sometime in the next two days, I caught the next available flight to Victoria, while Pat covered the home front.

During the afternoon hours of March 20—the welfare budget was coming up for debate that evening—I walked through the legislative building. As I strolled through the hallways, I was reminded of some of my previous walks through them, particularly one in 1953. At that time I was on my way to the office of then Superintendent of Child Welfare Ruby McKay. I was in Victoria to consult with her about my futile efforts to help a twelve-year-old runaway foster child, Jimmy. He had been physically abused and tortured by a stepfather, then severely beaten for bedwetting after being placed in a foster home in the Kootenays. He was moved into a loving foster home in my area—I was based in Salmon Arm at the time—but within a day or two of being placed there he ran away. He was picked up by the RCMP in Langley. Ruby was notified and in an action that was typical of her, she requested that I go to Langley, pick up Jimmy, and bring him back to Vernon with me. It was, she said, important for him to know that one person cared enough about him to find him and bring him back to a safe place.

Jimmy was glad enough to see me when I arrived in Langley. He seemed to enjoy our bus ride to New Westminster where we were to catch another bus that would take us back to Salmon Arm; however, when I turned my back briefly to speak to a ticket agent, he disappeared. Frantic, I phoned Ruby in Victoria to tell her the news. She requested that I come to Victoria; only when I arrived in her office did I realize that she was concerned not only about Jimmy's disappearance, but also with my feelings of failure over losing him.

As I walked the corridors in 1964, I remembered Ruby McKay and I remembered Jimmy. Bits and pieces of news about him had reached me over the years, none of them good. He had become a chronic runaway, following the pattern of so many other runaways in our care—a series of foster homes, then detention centres and reform schools, followed by several incarcerations for robbery. Finally in 1962 I read in a newspaper that he had been shot to death in an attempt to escape from a penitentiary in eastern Canada.

A feeling of failure always haunted me when I thought of Jimmy.

I was reminded of another time when I walked these same corridors. In 1956, when I was named District Supervisor of the Prince George welfare office, part of my orientation was a week in Victoria to meet with various department heads. On my last morning in the capital, I was sitting in a blue-carpeted office with lovely oak furniture and beautifully draped windows that looked out over manicured lawns. Platitudes were falling thick and fast from the mouths of several bureaucrats present concerning service to the community and the care and help our department was dispensing to the needy throughout the province.

As I listened I compared my surroundings to our office back in Prince George. It was an abandoned jail, in the basement of the old government building, which had been set on fire by an irate prisoner who wanted to move immediately to the new jail that was under construction a mile or two from the city centre. The prisoners were moved out, a few partitions were switched around, a coat of paint was slapped on, and these dingy quarters became our offices. As I sat in that spacious room in Victoria and listened to a veritable spate of self-serving bureaucratic utterances, I thought of the overworked staff back home, the lineups of clients waiting to be served. I thought of the unforgiving weather, the miserable driving conditions, the foster children at risk, the terrible poverty I had witnessed on my last visit to Stoney Creek Reserve and the massive indifference of the Indian Agent when I visited him, the growing number of unemployed men turning to welfare—I thought of these things as the platitudes tumbled in the air around me. And then I took a deep breath, sat up very straight in my upholstered chair, and shouted, "Balls!"

After a moment of stunned silence, the Minister of Welfare, Eric Martin, was brought in and I talked for the balance of the morning about how, in actual fact, welfare was functioning in the hinterlands. At noon, I was packed off to the airport, with pats on the back and numerous assurances that surely, inevitably, improvement would come.

Remembering those congenial pats on the back and the assurances of future improvement, I could only wonder that I, or someone like me, had waited too long to effectively say "Balls!" again to the whole welfare bureaucracy.

As I continued my walk through the legislature's halls, I gradually became aware that my presence that day was not universally welcome. I bumped into numerous government employees I had known from the past, but instead of the warm and sometimes affectionate greeting I might have expected, they seemed at a loss at how to deal with me, and anxious to avoid being seen with me. Almost without exception, they had only one question to ask of me: "How was your trip?" Before I could tell them that I had travelled not by dog team or snowshoes but by the most modern of aircraft, they had disappeared through the nearest exit.

If I was *persona non grata* with the civil servants, the reporters were willing, even anxious, to talk to me. In response to their questions, I said, "I have come down to try one more time to put pressure on the government to improve its welfare program."

It was probably a mistake for me to have remained in one place, the Prince George office, for ten years, I told them. "What happens is that the chickens come home to roost. The children I failed ten years before haven't disappeared—instead they grew up and they are on my caseload again. Now their problems have increased five and tenfold. The shortcomings in the service I witnessed ten years ago keep coming back to haunt me."

I repeated Roderick Haig-Brown's statement, "When we talk about one person now, we end up with all his children in the next generation," and illustrated his statement with the case history of a thirteen-year-old girl who had given evidence at her father's trial when he was charged with incest. The ordeal in court left her in a very distressed state; for lack of any treatment centre, she was placed in the girls' reform school. When she 'graduated' after two years, she was a confirmed alcoholic. Ten years after her incarceration, she had given birth to five children, all of them in foster homes.

"I don't see why this government doesn't understand that the failure of ten years ago is now costing the taxpayer thousands of dollars in support payments for these children," I told reporters, nor did I understand why taxpayers were not up in arms over such short-sighted and inhumane practices.

There are no words to describe the sensations that followed as I sat in the austere atmosphere of the legislature's public gallery while down below I heard myself being either defended or catistigated by one politician after another. There were moments when I felt that I was watching some kind of spectacle that had nothing whatsoever to do with me.

NDP MLA Alex MacDonald started the debate by demanding that I be rehired immediately.

"She is disloyal!" shouted Ernest Lecour, a Social Credit member from Delta. "That's why she was suspended!"

"Define it, you nuts!" roared the NDP's Tony Gragrave.

The speaker of the house rose and cautioned Gargrave about his language, which he withdrew.

"The suspension," said Wesley Black, "is an administrative problem. She has been told by the people I sent up into the area exactly what the solution is. When she's ready, willing, and able to abide by the situation, then she'll be reinstated. If she's not, she'll have to remain in the situation she is in now."

"Do you deny that you received a recommendation that she be fired?" an opposition member shouted.

"I deny that categorically," Black said. "The solution is in her hands and the administration's."

Opposition leader Robert Strachan stood up. "Will you tell us what are the conditions that she has to meet?"

"That's a matter between the individual concerned and the administration," replied the minister. "She was suspended under Section 67 of the Civil Service Act for misconduct. Mrs.

Moran has the right to appeal to the Civil Service Commission."

"Government policy on suspensions affect every civil servant," Tony Gargrave said. "They have a right to know what the
rules are. I demand an answer!"

"I've said all I'm going to say on the matter," replied Black.

"I've never heard such evasive conduct in my life!" said
Liberal Allan MacFarlane. "This is the most disgraceful and
arrogant situation we've run into here to date."

"We're making a fatal mistake," thundered North Vancouver Liberal Gordon Gibson. "We're throwing the blame and
firing a few privates—you should fire the general right at the
top!"

For an hour and thirty-six minutes, the wrangling, charges,
and countercharges were hurled back and forth across the floor
of the legislature. Then it was all over.

The Social Credit majority passed Wesley Black's budget and
approved his salary.

EIGHTEEN

Now began the struggle, first to be reinstated and then to return to work. For a few dark months, I found myself ill-equipped to carry on the vigorous campaign which might have ensured some semblance of victory—shortly after my March visit to the legislature, my health was causing concern. The continual nausea which was part of my pregnancy affected my liver; my doctor diagnosed hepatitis and recommended bedrest. This was no easy feat, with three active children in the family, seven years of age and under.

Although I would have denied the fact to anyone, I knew that I was depressed. The sense of purpose that was with me when I walked the hallways in Victoria faded in the weeks that followed as I struggled with poor health and a growing awareness that my employment as a provincial social worker might be at an end. Feelings of being adrift, of being useless, haunted me; I missed the work with my clients and my contact with the welfare office more than I could have believed possible. Over the years I had been off work on maternity leave or through illness, sometimes for months on end, but during those periods I had maintained contact with foster children, mothers on social assistance, old-age pensioners, and the like, and I had always been able to drop into the welfare office for a cup of coffee and a chat. Now I found the social service doors closed to me. I was not welcome in my old office, and I learned to avoid making contact with former clients, since such contact sometimes made difficulties for them. The media, lawyers, politicians, and supporters were still in the picture, but they didn't begin to make up for the people for were gone from my life.

In the last months of my pregnancy I fought against becoming bitter and neurotic, often a difficult struggle. There were moments when I felt betrayed. I wondered if my actions had been an exercise in futility as I watched the local welfare office carry on as if its workers had never signed a telegram, given interviews to the media, or threatened to go to Victoria if conditions did not improve. Sometimes I was sure that I heard a collective sigh of relief from Victoria as bureaucrats and politicians congratulated themselves that one more tempest in a teacup had been contained.

Nor was this all. In the early summer months of 1964, Pat left the jail service to open a mobile home sales business in the downtown area of Prince George, and overnight he had an active life away from the family. Increasingly I found that we were going in different directions, or more accurately, I remained in one spot wile Pat moved on. Admittedly a barfing wife, a tumultuous home life, and a never-ending struggle with an obdurate bureaucracy did not make for domestic bliss. Still, I felt that I had been deserted on every front. I felt very sorry for myself during those last months of my pregnancy.

Years before, I told my doctor that should I ever have sons, I would name them Pat and Mike. I already had my son Patrick. When my baby was born on September 9, 1964, Dr. Carson held up a squirming little mass of humanity in the delivery room and said, smiling, "Here's Mike!"

My health returned to normal immediately after Michael's

birth, and with it the courage and energy for the continuing struggle. However, first things first—we had to find a larger family home. In February of 1965, we finally left the trailer court and moved into a lovely old house overlooking the Fraser River on the hill leading out of South Fort George. Our house boasted an old cistern in what might euphemistically be called a basement, with sawdust for insulation and enough drafts so that even in the coldest weather we were never short of fresh air. Nevertheless, despite all kinds of inconveniences, it was a lovely family home. The fireplace built from rocks washed smooth by countless eons of river water burned brightly all through the winter, and in the heat of summer there was a screened-in verandah, tiger lilies in bloom, and raspberry canes just outside the back door for the picking.

When we moved into the house on the hill, I thought there was just a chance that, with my return to good health and our departure from the trailer court where our home had also served as an office, our life as a family—mother, father, children—might survive. Unfortunately, I found as year followed year, that although as a couple Pat and I still had our moments, that survival was not to be.

Letters—when I think of the weeks and months after my suspension, I see stacks of letters slipping through my mail slot.

My (unpaid) lawyer, Harry Rankin, was determined to force the government to give a definite reason for my suspension. Did my suspension result from the public wire to Jimmy Sadler? If so, I was no more guilty than the other four who signed it and were subsequently reinstated. Was I suspended because I wrote a letter to the premier and made it public? Was it my failure to promise to avoid the media in the future? Harry wondered if I could be kept under a present suspension for a possible future misdemeanor.

So, between Prince George and Vancouver and Victoria, the correspondence followed thick and fast.

On March 12, 1964, Rankin wrote to the Director of the Social Welfare Department: "You indicate in your letter of suspension that [Mrs. Moran] should be fully aware of the reasons for her suspension, but I am instructed that she is not aware of the reasons for her suspension and I would ask that you let me know the reasons. I take it that it might have been the letter addressed to W.A.C. Bennett. After having perused the letter, I see nothing in it that has not been amply demonstrated by many different people in the Social Welfare branch. Further to this suspension, I understand that all the workers in Prince George have been reinstated except Bridget Moran. I am now asking you to inform me of the reason for the distinction between Mrs. Moran's position and that of the other four workers . . . . "

In his reply of March 16, Deputy Minister E.R. Rickinson wrote: "I find it very hard to understand why Mrs. Moran advised you that she does not know the reason for her suspension. Mr. Burnham in personal interviews with Mrs. Moran in Prince George on two occasions outlined clearly to Mrs. Moran our reasons for this action."

Harry Rankin replied on March 23, posing two questions: "1. What is the reason for the suspension of Mrs. Moran? 2. Why has she not been reinstated when the other workers in the department have been reinstated?"

Back came a letter from the Deputy Minister, dated March 31, stating again that I knew the reason for my suspension, quoting Section 67 of the Civil Service Act and adding, "Her continued suspension is based on the fact that she would not give

Mr. Burnham her assurance that this unethical practice would not continue."

What surfaced out of all this was a choice of reasons for my suspension. We could take our pick: insubordination, making public communications to a civil servant, or failure to promise to stay away from the press. Finally, at the suggestion of the deputy minister, and in an attempt to cut through the morass that was developing, I filed a grievance through my lawyer with the Civil Service Commission. In that grievance I outlined the events to date. In response to this submission, I was startled to read that the Civil Service Commission had found yet another reason for my continued suspension—the Commission ruled that I had no legitimate grievance since I was not prepared "to honour the Oath of Office."

That was a shocker; suddenly my Oath of Office, never mentioned before, had come into play. I replied immediately through my lawyer that I had never been asked to promise to honour the Oath of Office which I had signed in Haney on December 20, 1951, and certainly I had never refused to honour it. Indeed, the Oath of Office had never been mentioned by Burnham, Rickinson, or anyone else in the ministry. Rebel though I was, I knew that I couldn't sign an oath and at the same time resolve not to honour it. Again through my lawyer I wrote to the Civil Service Commission. This letter pledged that I would honour my Oath of Office and I promised to resign if I found that I could not keep this pledge.

Finally on June 9, 1965, a year and four months after I was suspended, a decision reached me. The Chairman of the Civil Service Commission wrote to tell me he accepted my written commitment to honour my Oath of Office and advised me that my suspension as a part-time worker was lifted.

To begin with, there was great jubilation. Papers carried the headline, 'Bridget's Back On Her Own Terms.' "I will continue to make public statements about the welfare department," I told reporters. "However, I recognize that I cannot take an oath and then play fast and loose with it. I will abide strictly by my oath of office which means that I will not divulge information that comes to me through my employment. I have to add, however, that I have dozens of other sources of information available to me. I feel that this is a victory—no longer can a bureaucrat demand a promise from civil servants that they will never speak publicly about matters that concern them."

The next step was to inform the regional director Vern Dallamore that I was anxious to resume my career in social work at the point at which it was interrupted eighteen months before, working three days each week. I added, "I would appreciate a month or so to make arrangements to return to work, but should I be required sooner, I assure you that I am ready and willing to get into harness again."

Dallamore's response was brief: "I have no opening for a part-time worker in Prince George at this time and anticipate no vacancy in the future." Although with hindsight I should have seen the writing on the wall, I was still not prepared for it.

I was back to square one. There was no part-time job for me nor did it appear likely that there ever would be.

With four children, including a baby, a full-time job was out of the question. Besides, as Harry Rankin pointed out to the Civil Service Commission, "In my submission, Mrs. Moran is entitled to the job back that she was vacated from when this matter started . . . [The letter from Dallamore] is nothing short of discrimination. She is entitled to her seniority and her job back in the same position that she occupied prior to her suspension."

If this letter from Harry Rankin was ever answered, I have no record of it.

The only possibility left to me now was to sue the government, forcing them to return me to the work force. But could one sue the government? Yes, according to a number of lawyers I spoke to, supposing that the government will give you leave to sue. Couched in legalese, I was told that one had to obtain a fiat from the attorney-general's office in order to take the government to court. Pat and I tracked down Attorney-General Robert Bonner at a political meeting in Quesnel, and he assured us that I had been misinformed—anyone, he said, could sue any government. When I told the lawyers of this conversation with Bonner, they dared me to try it, and see how far I got.

Well, I was willing to give it a toss. Almost immediately I discovered that in order to start an action, which in the end might be impossible to start, I required several hundreds, perhaps thousands of dollars. The only money I had available to me were my Family Allowance cheques. I talked to the only two people I knew who had any money—one of them was the former publisher of the Prince George *Citizen*—and while they were sympathetic, they did not reach for their cheque-books.

In the end, everything petered out. My little rebellion tapered off into unanswered letters, unreturned phone calls. In 1966, two years after my letter to the premier, I had to face the fact that although it had been more difficult than Black or Sadler or Burnham had anticipated, the government had been able to dispense with my services without either firing me or forcing me to resign.

So be it, I thought. I'm not through yet. I will continue to comfort the afflicted and afflict the comfortable, whether I'm on a payroll or not!

NINETEEN

It was all very well to resolve to comfort the afflicted, but without a caseload such a resolution was nearly impossible to keep. I told myself that caring for a home and four young children was surely enough to keep any normal woman occupied, but no amount of self-chiding could keep me from missing the personal contact I had had over the years with the needy and the powerless. "The hand that rocks the cradle rules the world," said Phil Gaglardi when he was named Minister of Welfare. I wrote to him that although rocking the cradle had proved to be the most enriching experience of my life, I was rocking it full-time when I would have preferred to do it on a part-time basis.

But my main concern was not my continuing unemployment — from the beginning I had known that was a possibility— but was instead the necessity of keeping the welfare system's needs before the public and the mandarins in Victoria. In the years after my suspension my freelance articles about social services were published in the Vancouver *Sun*, the Prince George *Citizen*, and the now defunct Star Weekly. I appeared frequently on open line shows and for several years sat in the public gallery in the legislature when the welfare budget was debated. I had grown accustomed to the inevitable "How was your trip?" from civil servants in the legislative building, and missed the question when it was not forthcoming.

At the time of my suspension and for some years after, the only employer of social workers in Prince George was the provincial government. Finally a social service department was set up in the local hospital and in 1968 I was hired as a part-time worker. Unfortunately my unsettled marital state destroyed any sense of permanence I might have felt as I made the rounds in the hospital. I was off work for months when my marriage finally ended in divorce in 1969, and resigned when my children and I moved to Vancouver in 1971. I hoped that putting five hundred miles between Pat and me might ease some of the trauma of the divorce court.

At the time I intended the move to Vancouver to be permanent, but Prince George, with its wonderful variety in seasons, its openness and its aura of freedom, its sense of home, drew us back within a very few years.

In my years in Vancouver, I continued to press for changes in the welfare system. I helped to form a group called People on Welfare (known as POW!) and before long I was acting as an unofficial liaison between low income groups and the B.C. Association of Social Workers. It was inevitable that very soon after Gaglardi was named Minister of Welfare, his statements and his policies generated conflict with low income groups. Perhaps it was just as inevitable that in April 1972 I became part of that conflict.

In the spring session of the 1972 legislature Gaglardi brought forward Bill 49, a bill to amend the Social Assistance Act. Before this bill was passed into law the Social Assistance Act gave a client the right to appeal if a grant of money or services was reduced or refused. Procedures for setting up a tribunal were outlined in the act and its decisions were considered to be final. Almost as soon as Gaglardi took over Social Services he was in conflict with this 'right to appeal' section of the act. He tried first to declare findings of various ongoing tribunals to be merely recommendations which he could accept or ignore as he chose. When his interpretation was threatened with legal action, he proposed Bill 49, which would remove the right of appeal from the act altogether.

I sat on many welfare tribunals over the years. A fairly typical one concerned a man named Mike, his pregnant wife Sherry, and their two children. After many months on Social Assistance, Mike had been offered a construction job in a town in the central interior of British Columbia. He jumped at the chance to make a living wage, but after four days he left his employment, returned to his family, and applied to be reinstated on Social Assistance. He told his ministry worker that when he arrived on the construction site, he found that he would be working many feet above ground at the top of a tower. He said working conditions were unsafe; a man working beside him came within a hair's breadth of toppling off the structure. After witnessing this near-tragedy, Mike was gripped by the thought that his young wife would be in a terrible position if he fell from the tower and were maimed or killed. Panic-stricken, he turned in his equipment and returned home.

The social service worker took the position that he had refused employment, an absolute no-no in the ministry, and although his wife and children continued to receive assistance, he was not included in the grant. The worker's supervisor supported this ruling and Mike appealed. I acted for him, a social worker unconnected with the ministry acted for the department, and the two of us agreed to a third person, a priest with a very active social conscience. Needless to say our tribunal ruled that Mike be reinstated for Social Assistance until safe employment could be offered to him.

It was just this sort of case and ruling which challenged Gaglardi and drove him to his final solution—Bill 49.

A campaign had been waged for months to pressure Gaglardi into withdrawing or amending Bill 49. Social workers, lawyers, trade unionists, low income groups, church representative, politicians, all had protested the bill. An alternative Social Assistance Act had been drawn up and members of the government had been coerced into reading it, in the hope that at least some of the ruling Socreds would stray from the party line.

This lobbying failed to budge the government forces. Social Credit, with its overwelming majority in the House, supported Gaglardi and his bill. Loudly but ineffectively, Scott Wallace of the Conservatives and Dave Barrett of the NDP led the opposition to Bill 49 through the first and second readings. Responding to accusations that he was setting himself up as lord and master of welfare, Gaglardi, former machinist, former Minister of Highways, active minister of the Gospel, evangelist and sometime opera singer, said, "Who am I? I am a rather insignificant individual trying by the grace of God to help other people . . . this bill places me in control of a heavy responsibility."

"Mr. Gaglardi, you frighten me," Barrett said.

Word came through to us that the third and final reading of Bill 49 was on the order papers in the Legislature for the following afternoon. An emergency meeting was called in Vancouver — social workers, lawyers, clients, social activists, all gathered in what is now the Vancouver East Cultural Centre, but which was at that time a non-working church. Its galleries echoed that night to sounds of anger and frustration, as one plan of action after another was discussed and abandoned.

Finally it was decided that, partly because I had a car and was not employed, I would accompany five people from low income groups to Victoria the following day. We knew that we could not prevent the passage of Bill 49. All we could hope to do by some action of ours was to affirm our belief that people in need were entitled, not as a matter of charity, but as a matter of right, to financial assistance at a level that would ensure them a "reasonable, normal and healthy existence."

By some action of ours . . . but what action?

As the ferry plowed through the waters of Georgia Strait towards Victoria the following morning, we discussed possibilities over coffee in the restaurant. As we pondered and discarded one plan after another, I looked at the members of our hardy little band and thought, 'What a varied bunch of people we are!' There was the eldest among us, grey-haired Margaret, and beside her a young man who had known nothing but welfare cheques all his life. There were Caroline and Sharon from the Unemployed Citizen's Council, and Ian, an activist from a group called the Partisan Party. And there I was, an unemployed social worker.

What could we do, we questioned, to show our opposition to Bill 49? Sleep on the floor of the Legislative Buildings, so that legislators would have to step over us and talk to us? Perhaps, but we had no sleeping bags, and more to the point, some of us had young children waiting at home. Picket the Legislature? We were so pitifully few and besides, this had been done time without number. Stop somewhere in Victoria and buy locks and chains and attach ourselves to seats in the public gallery? Caroline favoured this plan, but those of us who were familiar with the gallery pointed out that at the very first rattle of a chain, we would be surrounded by security guards. This plan too was discarded.

Finally in desperation, as the ferry moved up to the dock, we decided that we would space ourselves around the gallery in the Legislature and call down to the legislators, one at a time. We would keep our language clean and direct no personal insults at Mr. Gaglardi—instead, we would attempt to make pertinent and succinct comments on the iniquity of Bill 49. It was decided that I would identify myself as a social worker and lead off the protest. We knew that an action such as we proposed would not stop passage of the bill, but we felt that we had to make one last gesture, however futile it might be.

So there we were on an afternoon in April 1972, the six of us scattered at strategic points in the public gallery of the Legislature in Victoria.

For forty-five tense minutes we listened to a long, rather pedestrian debate about the washout of a bridge on an access road somewhere between Watson Lake and Telegraph Creek. Finally after government members credited God and the inclement weather with the washout, and one Liberal and two New Democrats blamed the fiscal, recreational, and forestry policies of the Social Credit government for the destruction of the bridge, there was a pause. Then the Speaker of the House said, in a burst of speed, "I now call for the third and final reading of a bill to amend the Social Assistance Act therein after to be designated Bill Forty-Nine."

Mr Gaglardi, short, stocky, brown of skin and bright of eye, stood up. Then, another pause.

Thinking I might not get a chance, I leaped to my feet. My voice rang out over the startled legislators and came back to my ears: "I'm a social worker. I protest Bill 49 on the grounds that it is inhumane and probably illegal!"

Several things seemed to happen simultaneously.

The security guard, an old gentleman who was resting on the seat beside me, convinced that I didn't understand the rules of the public gallery, reached over, clamped a hand on my mouth and said, more in sorrow than in anger, "Here! Here! You're not allowed to make a noise!"

I made no attempt to resist his grip. Instead I turned my head so that my mouth was free of his hand and, because I couldn't think of another blessed thing to say, I took up my chant again: "I'm a social worker. I protest Bill 49 because . . . "

The old man took my arm. "Well then," he scolded, "you will have to come with me."

Meanwhile a voice was shouting, "Clear the galleries!"

Meanwhile, too, the voices of Ian and Sharon soared out over the gallery and, as my escort moved me towards a door, I had one brief and priceless glimpse of Margaret. Stout, grey-haired, she stood with her hands on her hips, looking all the world like a disgusted nanny, and shouted down to Gaglardi, "You're supposed to be helping people! Now, what do you say to that?"

As we navigated the steps towards the door at the end of the gallery, the escort released my arm and moved ahead of me. He stumbled. I clasped his shaking arm and asked, "Are you all right?"

He looked outraged as he shook off my hand and propelled me into a corridor.

Although I believed that I knew every twist and turn in the Legislative Buildings, that walk with my shaking and indignant guard seemed to lead endlessly through unfamiliar passages and hallways and around interminable corners. Finally we went through a door marked 'Sergeant at Arms.' Startled faces peered at us.

The old gentleman moved away from me.

"What is your name?" he asked. I told him.

"Keep her here," he said in an aggrieved voice and tottered out through the door.

I collapsed into the nearest chair and looked around. The startled faces were now recognizable as three men, one a young RCMP officer, the other two members of the security service. They studied me as closely as I surveyed them. Finally the eldest of the trio spoke. "What did you do?" he asked.

I told him.

As I talked a knowing look came into his eyes. When I had finished he spoke again. "Say," he said "you're not that woman from Prince George, are you?"

"I'm afraid I am."

He nodded, as if all was explained.

Time passed slowly. I wondered how my five companions had fared, and tried to guess what the authorities would do with me. The three men in the office spoke to each other, but so quietly that I couldn't make any sense of what they were saying.

Eventually two very large men came into the room. One of them said to me, "We are now going to escort you out of the building. You will not be allowed back in."

I had just enough ginger left in me to ask, "What do you mean, I will not be allowed back in? My taxes help pay for this building!"

"I mean," he said hurriedly, "that you will not be allowed back in today."

"That's all right then," I said. If the truth were known, I couldn't wait to leave. I had never engaged in an act of civil disobedience before; the exercise left me shaken and unnerved.

Outside I found my five companions surrounded by an army of reporters. They told me later that they were just beginning to wonder if I would need a lawyer. After I had answered a flurry of questions, I asked the reporters a question of my own: "Did Bill 49 pass the third reading?" Yes, I was told. The house adjourned for fifteen minutes after the galleries were cleared and soon after the sitting resumed, the bill passed its third and final reading.

As we walked away from the legislature, I silently cursed the futility of our actions, our lack of power. I had no way of knowing then that in less than six months, those Social Credit MLAs who looked so powerful as they swung around in their high-backed chairs would be sitting in opposition, and that one of the New Democratic Party's first acts as government would be to rescind Bill 49.

TWENTY

I could not have foreseen, when I was taken from the legislature in April 1972, that a new government would be in power within six months. Neither could I have imagined that nearly twenty years later, in March 1992, I would return to the legislature as an invited guest to attend the opening of the 35th Parliament of British Columbia, once again with a new government in charge. Ceremonies had not begun when I arrived for my spring visit in 1992 and I spent a few minutes walking the corridors again, looking at photographs of former premiers and their cabinets. I found a beautifully framed photo of W.A.C. Bennett, with the familiar figures of Gaglardi, Wesley Black, and Ray Williston close beside him. How indestructible they looked, standing next to their chief. As I roamed through the building, I almost expected to see Ruby McKay or Amy Leigh or Bob Burnham emerge from one of the inner offices, and I thought that surely someone would walk up to me and ask, "How was your trip?"

Much had happened in the twenty years since I was escorted from the legislature. On the political scene the New Democratic Party under Dave Barrett had taken over the reins of power for a brief thirty-nine months, only to have the Socreds slip back with a majority, this time with another Bennett, Bill, as premier.

That same year, 1975, we returned to Prince George. We moved into a house owned by my ex-husband Pat—he proved to be a generous landlord—and I picked up the pieces of my life where I had dropped them four years earlier. It came as something of a shock to discover that in those years away from Prince George my family, like swallows too big for their nest, had begun to spread their wings and were preparing to fly away. Mayo and Roseanne left for Vancouver to attend university in the fall of 1976; Patrick and Michael were in high school. With our number reduced from five to three, the house suddenly seemed to the boys and me to be empty and quiet, too quiet.

And in 1977, quite unexpectedly, since I had just turned fifty-four and considered myself to be over the hill job-wise, I found employment. For the first time in thirteen years I had work which included a caseload and a full paycheque—I was hired as a social worker by the Prince George School District.

For many years the school district had been employing social workers and psychologists. In 1977, a new entity, the regional team, came into being. As an essential part of Special Education, this new concept was designed to ensure that each of the seventy-plus schools scattered over one of the largest school districts in the province was covered by a psychologist, a social worker, and a speech pathologist, working as a team with the school, students, families, and all available community agencies.

From my first day on the job until I retired in 1989, I was doing my kind of social work. The only authority I had, the only powers, were the powers of persuasion I exercised to encourage parents and students to work with me. I had nothing to do with granting money, moving children from one home to another, or any of the other duties usually associated with welfare work. The referrals I received as part of a regional team ran the gamut from academic difficulties through problems of in-school behaviour, the detection and reporting of physical abuse, intervening in students' families when problems of health, violence, poverty, or unemployment surfaced, and, especially in the years as we moved toward the 1990s, dealing with the sexual abuse of children. Once again I was making home visits, sitting at kitchen tables and sipping tea while families from every strata of Cariboo society worked with me to solve problems, make their lives better, and sometimes, ease their pain.

In summer and winter I was on many of the same roads I had travelled as a much younger woman, visiting schools and making calls far beyond the reach of my office in Prince George. I worked for the school district for twelve years; in those years I never lost the wonderful feeling that I was back where I belonged.

As a school district employee I was often an advocate, an intermediary, between the families on my caseload and my former employer, the Social Service Ministry. I discovered that in the years since my work with that ministry, resources in the welfare and mental health fields had been developed beyond anything we had hoped for in the days of W.A.C. Bennett and Wesley Black; I also found that, as in the bad old days, too many people, adults and children, continued to fall through the net provided by the social service system.

In my work with the school district I was in regular contact with the ministry—perhaps I was calling about a six-year-old boy who had no jacket on a cold winter's morning, or maybe it was a child whose stepfather had pointed a gun at her the night before, or again it might concern a single mother who was being threatened with eviction form her home. My reports, my requests for service, confirmed what I had long suspected about the welfare system: it had not become kinder or more efficient in the thirteen years during which I was removed from almost all direct contact with welfare recipients; it had just become bigger.

Statistics confirm this fact. At the present time in British Columbia there are just under 250,000 people living on welfare, a figure that includes 86,574 children, 39,220 single parents (almost all of them women), and 17,885 disabled people. Sadly, too, there are over 6,200 children in some kind of foster care in the province. It is estimated that up to seventy-five percent of these children come from economically deprived homes. Not included in these figures are the many thousands of people, eighty percent of them women, working for minimum wage, which leaves them and their families living far below the poverty line.

When large numbers of people are living below the poverty line, whether on social assistance, working for minimum wage, or in receipt of some kind of pension, one can be sure that a very large bureaucracy is not far behind. So it is in British Columbia. The provincial Ministry of Social Services now employs nearly 4,500 workers, exclusive of clerical staff, fulfilling the roles with which the public is familiar—financial assistance workers, social workers, rehabilitation officers, inspectors, supervisors, managers, and directors.

This, however, is only the tip of the iceberg. There is another social service empire in the shadow of the ministry, 10,400 workers strong, which is employed to deliver a variety of services in communities across the province but which is not directly on the ministry's payroll. This surrogate social services delivery system began in a small way through non-profit organizations

in the last years of W.A.C. Bennett's regime. Money was chan-
nelled into groups at the community level to provide needed
services. Perhaps it was a Homemakers Society, which put
homemakers into a family when the mother was hospitalized, or
into old age pension homes to keep seniors functioning outside
of institutions. Or a grant may have been made to a Special
Services to Children Society which brought together needy or
disturbed children and child care workers.

Following the initiative begun under the elder Bennett, private businesses, along with various non-profit groups, were set
up at an increasing pace throughout the 1970s and 1980s to meet
perceived community needs and to share in the money flowing
in larger and larger amounts from the ministry. From small
beginnings, this non-traditional social welfare system has produced a shadow ministry with more than double the employees
of the ministry itself. Sometimes the process is called privatiz-
ing, sometimes contracting out, at other times it is described as
the purchasing of services. It has almost as many modes of
operation as there are societies and companies. Either through
non-profit community groups or through entrepreneurial organizations, this army of 10,400 work with sexual abusers or their
victims, the mentally or physically handicapped, pensioners of
all kinds, juvenile delinquents, wife batterers, substance abusers,
and non-functional children and adults; these same 10,400 are
assessing, treating, counselling, caring, containing, controlling,
befriending. They are everywhere and they are providing many
of the services which once belonged in the special fiefdom of the
social worker.

This para-ministry is big business in the province. Despite the
fact that several of its organizations pay wages just above minimum wage (many non-profit societies are limited through a lack
of funding, while the private companies view their delivery of

service as a business venture with profit the objective), this shadow group within the social service system cost B.C.'s taxpayers $492 million in 1991.

During its many years in power, Social Credit repeatedly declared that it was not in government to create a welfare state. Even while that declaration was being sounded, Socred social policies ensured that a welfare state was in the making. The citizens of the British Columbia welfare state—social assistance recipients, foster children, and those minimum wage earners, unemployed workers and pensioners living below the poverty line—now total nearly one-third of the province's population. Add to that number the 15,000 workers who are, either directly or indirectly, on the payroll of social services, and one realizes that the welfare state operating within the provincial body politic is massive, cumbersome and growing.

EPILOGUE

It is impossible to speak of a social services system without also speaking of poverty. Any reform of that system begins and ends with a recognition that too many people, especially women and children, live and die in a state of poverty in our society. Sadly, the disadvantaged provide much of the material which ensures that welfare offices, jails, clinics, treatment centres, and foster homes will continue to flourish and multiply.

Poverty means many things to many people.

To some it is linked with drunkenness, immorality, shiftlessness, depravity. This view is at least as old as the bible itself. One of the Proverbs tell us: "The drunkard and the glutton shall come to poverty: the drowsiness shall clothe a man with rags." With this biblical prophecy as its basis, a mythology has evolved in which the poor, given a choice between independence and dependence, have always opted for dependence. The needy embrace their poverty, we are told, because they are lazy, corrupt, slow-witted, irresponsible. In this view poverty has everything to do with character and moral fibre and nothing whatever to do with money.

There is another, simpler, theory of poverty.

Author, comedian and activist Dick Gregory, in his book *Nigger*, tells of running to his mother as a little boy of six, and crying to her, "The kids are teasing me. They're saying we're poor." "We're not poor," his mother assured him, "we're just broke."

Dick Gregory's mother was right. Despite all the myths that have been developed around it, poverty is simply a lack of money for the necessities of life. A shortfall in money over a period of time results in poor health, low energy levels, chronic anxiety, under-education, and too often, anger expressed in anti-social behavior and substance abuse. These are the results of poverty, however, not its cause, as so many of our politicians and leaders would have us believe. And since poverty is nothing more nor less than a lack of money, it follows that only money can solve this economic plague.

Unfortunately Canadian society, in common with most societies around the world, has never accepted the truth about the causes of poverty, nor its solutions. In the forty years during which I have been involved in the welfare game, one approach after another has been tried, every one of them designed to curb a welfare system which we are told is out of control. I have watched Social Credit governments in British Columbia, for example, follow a program of punitive measures, ostensibly to reduce dependency: welfare rates and the minimum wage are set far below the poverty line; mothers of young children are forced out of the home to look for work; fringe benefits such as health care, dental services, help with education or training are restricted or cancelled altogether, along with extra recreational facilities for children; more and more officials are hired to search out fraud, malingering, or 'questionable' relationships such as that between a single mother living on welfare and a male friend. These harsh measures always remind me of my proud Irish mother in the dirty thirties answering to the village council because she managed to buy a small radio with money she earned taking in laundry. Then, as now, the measures divised by authorities to harass and demean the disadvantaged were legion.

Needless to say, jurisdictions are not always ogres, determined to keep the poor in their perceived place; sometimes other less negative approaches will be attempted. There will be more and better day care facilities, retraining programs will be set up, higher earnings will be allowed within the social assistance regulation, the welfare rates and the minimum wage will be raised a few percentage points, and community grants will be bestowed, all of which add brighter dimensions to the lives of the elderly, handicapped, and single parents and their families.

However, no matter how the agencies have proceeded, victory in the war against poverty remains as elusive as ever. I recognized this grim fact yet again when I began my employment with the school district in 1977. Scattered throughout my list of cases, I read the names of some of the descendants of Nancy and William, about whom I had talked so endlessly at the time of my suspension. Whether the approach of the bureaucrats was punitive or humane, little difference could be detected in the end result for Nancy and William, or for their descendants—whatever the current social philosophy in vogue, the majority of those descendants have ended up on the welfare rolls and in clinics or institutions of some kind.

In the mid-1960s, the study of Nancy and William's family tree took us into the third generation with over 100 names on its branches. At that time our study indicated that at least eighty percent of the descendants were dependent on government funding; there was continuing illiteracy, poor housing, poor health, and a repeating pattern of anti-social behaviour, such as wife battery, gang rape, armed robbery, drunken driving, and manslaughter.

Sad to say, as a school district employee working with the children for whom Nancy and William are now great-grandparents and great-great-grandparents, I found the same desperate conditions and lamentable statistics: eighty percent were dysfunctional in the very areas which we had documented years before. There was one difference, however—whereas in the 1960s there were 100 descendants, approximately eighty of whom were dysfunctional, the family tree twenty years later lists well over 1,000 names, with 700 or 800 in social or financial distress. If present social policies continue unchanged, it is not difficult to forecast that this family will produce not just hundreds, but thousands, of dependent anti-social individuals in the next forty years.

And this is only one family constellation. There are hundreds, thousands, in similar circumstances across the country.

Billions of dollars have been spent on band-aid remedies to alleviate poverty. The one approach that has never been tried is the granting of sufficient money to ensure that every individual in Canada has a standard of living above the poverty line. Nothing else will do; nothing else will work.

This approach is the guaranteed annual income system or the negative income tax. It is not new in Canada. We already have limited guaranteed annual income systems in the forms of Family Allowance for children and Old Age Security for seniors. These grants are issued with a minimum of regulations; being Canadian, and simply being born in one case, or reaching the age of sixty-five in the other, is sufficient to ensure eligibility. When Family Allowance or Old Age Security benefits are paid into households in which the income is above a certain level, either a portion or all of the allowance or pension money is taxed (or more familiarly, clawed) back by the government. These two plans are the simplest and least expensive programs that operate at present in the social service spectrum.

Lacking from both Family Allowance and Old Age Security, however, is one vital element—neither program is adequate. Family Allowance alone is insufficient for the needs of a child; an individual of sixty-five requires Old Age Security to be subsidized by superannuation, Canada Pension, savings, or a supplemental grant. It is this inadequacy which has caused anti-poverty groups to reject the guaranteed annual income out of hand. Quite correctly these groups state that unless a guaranteed income is also sufficient to meet needs, the disadvantaged would be no better off then they are now.

If, however, the concept of adequacy is incorporated into a guaranteed annual income system, the following would apply— just as everyone sixty-five and over in Canada receives Old Age Security and every child in Canada receives Family Allowance, under a guaranteed annual adequate income system, a targeted block of the population (probably single-parent families as a start) would receive a monthly cheque in an amount above the poverty line—presently an individual or family is considered to be living below the poverty line if food and housing consume sixty percent or more of available income. And just as the government takes back via income tax Old Age Security or Family Allowances paid to people with incomes in excess of a stated amount, so it would, under the guaranteed income, take back a percentage in high income situations. Starting with one group (perhaps, as I suggested, the single parent families as the neediest), the system would then be extended to other blocks of disadvantaged citizens as they were identified.

There is no lack of politicians and professionals who insist that the country cannot afford such a system. The answer, of course, is that we cannot afford not to have such a system. The money needed is available to begin a real war on poverty. All that is lacking is a commitment on the part of governments to engage the enemy. A good beginning would be an end to funds spent on programs which are doomed to failure, and a fairer and more equitable collection and distribution of tax dollars.

Sometimes as I listen to the leaders in our society, I think that the Two Nations I found in British Columbia forty years ago, the powerful and the powerless, will always be with us, and that the powerful will, indeed, inherit the earth. And then I remember my early days as a social worker and recall many of our policies and actions which were acceptable then, but which would never be tolerated now: the pressure we exerted on unmarried mothers to place their babies for adoption, the pittance paid to seniors and then only when they were seventy years old, the Native children we uprooted from their reserves and, without a qualm, placed in alien environments. I remember the judgements and the prejudices we took with us into disadvantaged homes—and as I remember, I realize that there have been tremendous changes in philosophies and systems, and that that process of change is continuous.

Perhaps, after all, the powerful will not inherit the earth.

I think these long thoughts and inevitably my mind slips back in time.

I see myself, age twenty-eight, tall and very slim, with red hair and freckles, leaving the Canadian Pacific Railway Station in Vancouver. It is November 4, 1951, and as I peer through the mist that hangs over Cordova Street I ask myself, "I wonder what the future holds for me here in British Columbia?"

 BRIDGET MORAN is the author of *Stoney Creek Woman: The Story of Mary John* and *Judgement at Stoney Creek*, both published by Arsenal Pulp Press. Now retired, she lives in Prince George, B.C.

SELECTED TITLES FROM
ARSENAL PULP PRESS

The Imaginary Indian   *Daniel Francis*
A fascinating and revealing history of the image of the Indian as
mythologized by Canadian culture, propagating stereotypes of the
"Noble Savage" that exist to this day. *$15.95*

Children of the First People   *Dorothy Haegert*
A moving collection of photographs of the Native children of
Canada's west coast, along with narratives by ten Native Elders,
speaking eloquently about their own childhoods. *$21.95*

Resistance and Renewal   *Celia Haig-Brown*
The first book to deal frankly and openly with the painful legacy of
Indian residential schools in Canada, based on interviews with former
students of the Kamloops Indian Residential School. Winner of the
B.C. Book Prize. *$11.95*

Judgement at Stoney Creek   *Bridget Moran*
The heart-wrenching story of the divisive inquest into the hit-and-run
death of a young pregnant Carrier Native in central British Columbia,
and an analysis of how Canada's justice system has failed aboriginal
people. *$12.95*

Stoney Creek Woman   *Bridget Moran*
The bestselling biography of Mary John, a remarkable Carrier Native
and mother of twelve living on the Stoney Creek reserve in central
British Columbia: a slice of B.C. history from a unique woman's
perspective. *$9.95*

Available from your local bookstore, or prepaid (add $1.00 per book
for postage + 7% GST) directly from:

ARSENAL PULP PRESS
100-1062 Homer Street
Vancouver, BC Canada V6B 2W9

Write for our free catalogue.